A TWISTED CASE OF MURDER

Mrs. Lillywhite Investigates
BOOK EIGHT

EMILY QUEEN

A Twisted Case of Murder

ISBN- 978-1-953044-90-7

First Edition

Printed in the U.S.A.

Table of Contents

Chapter One 1

Chapter Two 16

Chapter Three.. 22

Chapter Four.. 31

Chapter Five 39

Chapter Six 50

Chapter Seven 60

Chapter Eight... 67

Chapter Nine 76

Chapter Ten... 86

Chapter Eleven 97

Chapter Twelve 101

Chapter Thirteen 109

Chapter Fourteen 117

Chapter Fifteen... 126

Chapter Sixteen 134

Chapter Seventeen.. 146

Chapter Eighteen.. 154

Chapter Nineteen 162

Chapter Twenty 173

Chapter Twenty-One 180

Chapter Twenty-Two... 194

Chapter Twenty-Three..206

Chapter Twenty-Four 217

Chapter Twenty-Five 226

Chapter Twenty-Six 236

Chapter Twenty-Seven 251

CHAPTER ONE

Whack, whack, whack!

Rosemary Lillywhite tightened her grip on the handle of the three-pronged instrument, raised her arm, and swung it back down again just as hard as she could. She felt a thrill of satisfaction trail up her spine as it sunk, easily, into its intended target. Once, twice, three times more, she repeated the motion until finally, there was no doubt—the messy and, to any sane person, unpleasant— job was finished.

She smiled a slow, delicious smile that failed to fade even when she noticed the state of her fingernails, caked with black as they were. Instead of causing concern, the sight prompted a wry chuckle. Rosemary threw the death-dealing soil cultivator aside and stood, brushing the dirt from her dress while thinking that she probably ought to have donned an apron or at least a pair of gloves.

That, however, would have required forethought, and

today's endeavor was one of spontaneity. Next time, Rosemary promised herself, she'd dress appropriately— and there was certain to be a next time, of that she was sure. It was too much of a thrill, one she wanted to repeat again and again.

It wasn't surprising, really. Once one got a taste, a dalliance could soon lead to obsession—or so she'd heard from a reliable source.

Having tested her hand, Rosemary found she understood what all the fuss was about. She couldn't quite call herself a gardener, not at this early stage, but she'd taken to the new hobby with gusto.

Clearing a patch of weeds and exposing the rich, dark soil underneath elicited the same feeling of anticipation she felt when attaching a new canvas to her easel. Rosemary imagined watching the empty space fill with colorful blooms would be just as satisfying as applying the final brush stroke.

She squatted low now, a motion that only a few weeks ago would have been possible but not entirely comfortable, and began to scoot a sizable evergreen shrub inch-by-inch towards the readied hole.

"Come on. We can do this. Just a bit of cooperation," she told the shrub. Ariadne Whittington, mother to Rosemary's beau, Max, had assured her that any gardener worth their salt talked to their plants and felt no shame in the least for doing so.

Rosemary's own mother would never concede that point, and that was why, in part, she had failed to fill Evelyn in on her new pastime. She knew for certain her mother would loathe the fact that sometimes, Rosemary wore the same trousers from her calisthenics sessions out into the garden. It was, after all, Rosemary's own private space. Why shouldn't she feel comfortable in it?

Everything from the dirty fingernails to the mere mention of *calisthenics sessions* would have caused her mother a coronary—or, at the very least, caused Evelyn to accuse her daughter of trying to *give* her a coronary.

"Ahem." Suddenly, Rosemary heard the unmistakable sound of her butler clearing his throat and whirled around in expectation of the exasperated expression she felt certain would be painted across his face. If Wadsworth was one thing, it was a traditionalist, just like Evelyn. While Rosemary had concluded she rather enjoyed taking care of herself, Wadsworth preferred his mistress allow the staff to tend to her every need.

Rosemary's ideas regarding independence, however, were neither here nor there at that very moment because on Wadsworth's arm posed a ravishing figure of a woman veritably vibrating with excitement.

"Rosie!" the vision screeched uncharacteristically, careening herself in Rosemary's direction. She thought, for a moment, that Vera might leap straight over the wheelbarrow resting halfway between them, but she sidestepped it deftly and swept Rosemary into her arms.

"I missed you so much Frederick packed our cases halfway through the holiday! He declared me far too droll in your absence and insisted that if we ever do a second honeymoon, you'll be forced to come along and book an adjoining suite!" Vera practically shouted into her dearest friend's hair.

"My brother is far smarter than I'd given him credit for, then," Rosemary replied, squeezing Vera back with relief. The knot that remained lodged in her throat anytime one of her loved ones strayed too far from England finally loosened, the sudden absence of it bringing a sting of tears to her eyes. "From now on, we travel together, or not at all," she agreed.

Vera leaned back and gazed at Rosemary for a long moment, her eyes searching for signs of distress. An image of Rosemary from one year prior swam up as it still often did, one of a woman broken by loss and one that—thank the gods—bore little resemblance to the woman standing before her now. She breathed a sigh of relief, and then cocked an eyebrow.

This Rosemary didn't even look like the one she'd left behind last month. Her shoulders were straighter and more toned, making her neck appear longer and more regal. The long blond locks remained, despite Vera's insistence her friend ought to give in to the current styles and affect a smart bob like her own, but there was a brightness to Rosemary's eyes that hadn't been there before. There was also a smudge of dirt on her cheek that further widened Vera's grin.

"What in heavens have you been doing, Rosie?" she asked, her gaze traveling around the garden with more interest now.

Rosemary linked arms with Vera, steered her towards a bank of meticulously groomed rose bushes, and explained.

"You see, we've had a bit of trouble with the trellis and the seating beneath it. The whole thing was crawling with deathwatch beetles! Just after you and Frederick departed, the trellis let go and came tumbling down. It took the potting shed with it, but that had rotted as well, and now, here we are."

Rosemary's home in the neighborhood of Marylebone, a moderately affluent area of northwest London, was one in a strip of attached townhouses. In an attempt to provide privacy to each occupant, every home featured its own bit of garden, separated from its neighbors on either side by rows of tall hedges.

Wooden fencing stretched across the rear of the properties, bordering a section of communal grass referred to by the residents as 'the park', but not to be confused with the much larger Regent's Park slightly further east.

At the head of the common sat a quaint stone church.

Rosemary enjoyed a lovely view of the spire rising above the treeline from her garden terrace and could hear the big copper bell ringing out each hour in dulcet tones.

Vera jabbed Rosemary in the ribs gently with her elbow and quipped, "So you've decided to loosen the purse strings and redo the entire garden. I heartily approve, and it looks positively smashing. Should I assume, based on the size of your arm muscles, that you tore down the crumbling potting shed and rebuilt it with your own two hands?"

Out of reflex and a feeling of elation at her friend's return, Rosemary flexed against Vera's hand in a mock masculine gesture, eliciting a laugh and a further raised eyebrow.

She gestured towards the portion of fencing that ran along the rear edge of the property. "There's a small crew of workmen taking a break in the park on the other side of the fence. I've just been dallying out here, but I have come to find I rather enjoy it. As for my arm muscles, you've Ivy Gibson and Esme Prescott to blame—really, the entire LLV and their relentless exercise sessions."

"So the London Lady Vigilantes are at it again, are they?" Vera asked, amused at her cleverness.

"Don't call them that to their faces," Rosemary warned. "It's the Ladies for London Vitality, and Ivy

Gibson is taking the whole thing quite seriously. I doubt she'll find your sense of humor amusing."

Vera shrugged off the warning. "You've been quite busy, haven't you?" she asked, shaking her head. "You even ensured Freddie and I came home to a clean house. We've nothing whatsoever to fret over; you thought of everything, down to the new bedsheets. You're a marvel, Rosie, truly."

It was true; Rosemary had ensured her brother's new home was appropriately unpacked and organized, but even so, she brushed off Vera's effusive praise.

"I've an excess of staff for little old me," she said, an undercurrent of irritation evident in her tone. Whether it had to do with the *reason* she found herself living in the large townhouse by herself or something else Vera couldn't say, but she expected her friend would come out with it eventually. Rosemary tended to hold things in until they sprang forth in a flurry, while Vera practiced a method of simply bursting at the seams a little bit each day.

"Anna was perfectly happy to organize and simultaneously admire your wardrobe," Rosemary continued. "I suspect she's bragged to all her friends for being entrusted with *the* Vera Blackburn's shoe collection."

The part of Vera that was, ultimately, quite vain found Rosemary's statement rather endearing and vowed to bestow a gift upon Rosemary's young maid so that she might become the object of even further envy amongst her young friends.

"She's a doll for it," was what Vera said aloud and with complete sincerity.

"You did have a lovely time on your holiday, I hope?" Rosemary asked, bending over to pull a weed from between two delphiniums. "Aside from missing me terribly, of course."

Vera grinned and nodded, her eyes clouding with the haze of young love and newlywed bliss. "The loveliest," she confirmed. "Mallorca was positively divine. We lounged on the beach for days on end and then danced until dawn. I wish we hadn't had to return to London at all, if I'm honest." Her voice turned wistful now. "Everything seems so…different."

"You're no longer a bride. Now, you're a wife," Rosemary said, understanding without requiring any further explanation, "and that's a role you'd decided you would never play. It's only to be expected you might require a moment—maybe even two—to adjust to it all."

They walked, arm-in-arm, a little further while Vera contemplated her friend's statement. "You're right, of course, but also—and this will come as no shock—it's your mother," she finally admitted, exasperation evident in her tone. It was not, by far, the first time Vera, or any number of people, for that matter, had made the same exclamation.

"We've barely returned from our honeymoon, and already she's sent someone by to measure the guest bedroom and determine the size cot to get for her next grandchild. She nearly went into a convulsive fit when Freddie told her we weren't planning on trying for a baby just yet. She's certifiable; you know that, don't you?"

"Of course, dear," Rosemary replied, "and unless you've been living in blissful ignorance all these years, so did you."

Vera's marriage to Rosemary's brother Frederick might be shiny and new, but as her oldest and dearest friend, Vera had been on intimate terms with the entire Woolridge family practically since birth.

Vera wasn't daft, either. She was a good egg, smart and resourceful, loyal to a fault, and exceptionally adept at getting what she wanted. Until that is, she'd begun going toe-to-toe with Evelyn Woolridge on the regular.

"Seeing her tramp all over you lot is one thing," Vera replied. "Her butting into our childbearing plans is quite another." She stopped short and sent a pained, contrite look towards Rosemary. "I'm sorry. I shouldn't complain overly much, should I?"

Rosemary smiled thinly and patted Vera's hand. It all felt so long ago now. She was still a young woman, well within childbearing age, and by her mother's way of thinking should be leading around a passel of little ones by now.

Evelyn—after feeling scandalized, of course—would be interested to know it hadn't been for lack of trying. Rosemary's late husband had desired a son, and she had desperately wanted to give him one.

Except, it hadn't happened, and Rosemary had no idea why. The doctors didn't, either; it just worked out that way sometimes, they'd said, before shooing her out of their offices. Eventually, she had decided that perhaps it simply wasn't meant to be.

"*My* mother isn't helping, either," Vera went on. "They have both quite lost their minds. Furthermore, they seem to have joined forces with even more solidarity than usual. Upon arriving home, I found a pair of hand-crocheted baby booties waiting for me! It's far too soon for that sort of talk. Freddie and I haven't even settled in, and if I get cast in this play, there's no telling how long it might run…."

She stopped walking and talking and took a deep breath. "I'm sorry," she said again, calmer now. "I shouldn't be so angry or surprised at all. I merely expected that first would come the hints, increasing in frequency but delivered with smiles, and *then* the more obvious shove in the direction of the nursery shops."

While listening to Vera's diatribe, Rosemary gathered a pair of gloves and a bucket from the terrace that butted up to the back of the house. She now led her friend to the far end of the garden.

There, during the initial survey of the property, Rosemary had found a flat slab of slate sunk into the topsoil, which had turned out to be part of a path the earth had all but swallowed.

The workmen had dutifully pulled and reset each piece, cleaned up and mulched the planting beds where Rosemary arranged a series of bird baths and houses. To her delight, they had already begun to attract some adorable little forest friends.

One of the baths, made of alabaster, featured an ornate sculpture of a songbird bending over to take a drink, its tail feather pointed towards the sky. It was Rosemary's favorite piece, not only because it was beautifully made but also because she enjoyed watching the real birds try to fight the artificial one.

"What are you doing with a bucket of"—Vera crinkled her nose—"what is that in there? Kitchen scraps?"

Rosemary laughed. "It's food for the birds. Gladys sets aside anything they'll eat—fruits that have started to turn, vegetable peelings, nuts—and I bring it out each morning. Today I got caught up with the planting, and they're becoming impatient. Hear them chattering?"

Vera did, indeed, hear the noise Rosemary described, but to her ear, it sounded more like squawking than chattering. She raised one eyebrow but dutifully followed Rosemary, recoiling in disgust when she saw not a flock of bluebirds but a pair of crows hopping around the footpath.

"Oh, no!" Vera said with a shudder, "you've been invaded by crows. Dirty, disgusting things." She kicked a foot in their general direction and shouted, "Shoo! Shoo!"

Rosemary hushed her friend. "For heaven's sake, don't frighten them!" she said while one of the crows cocked its head to one side and peered suspiciously at Vera. "I've been feeding them for weeks and they've only just begun to trust me."

"Why on earth would you want to do that?" Vera demanded. "What reason could you possibly have to purposefully invite harbingers of evil into your garden?"

"That's a bit dramatic, don't you think?" Rosemary replied. She stepped gingerly towards the two inky black birds, holding the bucket of foodstuffs out in front of her. The crows hopped around and kept their beady eyes trained on the bucket. "It's nonsense besides," Rosemary continued. "They're actually quite clean and are far smarter than most people think—they're simply scavengers and so have garnered a poor reputation for their tendency to congregate around dead bodies."

As there was nothing else to be done, Vera tolerated the lecture. Only the barest hint of a raised brow gave away her sardonic mood.

"In point of fact," Rosemary informed her audience of one, "crows are monogamous creatures, and they become tightly bonded with their flock, like a family. They even talk with one another. Can't you hear it? They're nervous but curious about the scraps. It may sound dramatic, but that's what I think."

The larger bird, the one Rosemary presumed to be the male, hopped sideways over to his partner and lowered his head. She, in turn, began grooming his neck with her beak.

"Isn't that sweet?" Rosemary asked, to which Vera replied with a dubious glance. "She's preening the spots he can't reach. They're mates."

Vera's lips quirked, and she peered at her friend with a wrinkled brow. "I really ought not to have left you here all by your lonesome, Rosie. You have, quite literally, gone to the birds!"

Rosemary ignored the proclamation with a roll of her eyes and instead focused on the two crows who accepted her offering with a racket that, to Vera at least, still sounded like nothing but noise.

A moment later, the three members of the work crew and their supervisor, returning from their lunch break, emerged from the gate at the back of the garden. One of the men gazed towards Vera with some interest, but after a pointed look from their supervisor, quickly averted their eyes. The second avoided acknowledging Rosemary entirely, and he, she suspected, fully disapproved of her inclination to participate in the landscaping process.

Only one of the workers approached Rosemary and Vera, albeit with some hesitation. He was a hulking, brutish man with an unexpectedly soft smile, and Rosemary greeted him warmly despite the supervisor's narrow-eyed expression. She was, after all, the lady of the house and, ultimately, the one in charge.

"Hello, Jack," Rosemary said with a smile.

Suddenly, the birds stopped in their tracks, their caws becoming short, clipped, and urgent as they swooped out of the garden and up, up to land beneath the eave of the church steeple and the safety of the nest tucked beneath it. They peered down at Jack with suspicion and cawed once more.

"Miss Rose," he replied, raising one club of a hand and presenting her with a fragile-looking bellflower, his eyes shifting uncertainly in Vera's direction. "Stem got bent," he stammered. "Didn't want it to go to waste. Best put it in some water, though. Won't last long in this heat."

Graciously, Rosemary accepted the gift. "Thank you. It's quite beautiful. Jack, this is Vera, my dear friend and now my sister-in-law," she explained just as the supervisor hollered, "Come on, now, Jack, you've got work to do. The mice in those traps aren't going to drown themselves, are they?"

Rosemary grimaced at the thought, but Jack merely nodded politely in Vera's direction and, before steam began to pour from his supervisor's ears, ambled across the lawn.

"You always do make the most unlikely friends, Rosie dear," Vera said after he'd gone, linking arms with Rosemary once more and steering her back towards the house.

"It is rather a rare talent of mine," Rosemary replied.

Chapter Two

"Now, let's go get something to eat. I'm famished. Is there still breakfast?" Vera wanted to know.

"I'm positive we can convince Gladys to scrounge up something," Rosemary assured with a smile, "but we'd better hurry. There's an LLV meeting this morning, and I don't want to be late."

At that, Vera brightened. "I'd like to see for myself what the Vigilantes are up to. I think I'll accompany you if it's quite all right." Without waiting for an answer, she continued, "I'll just nip a slice of toast from the kitchen and then pop back home to change."

She attempted to trot happily off only to be intercepted by a slip of a woman who'd emerged, as if out of nowhere, through a narrow break in the hedge.

At the same time, Dash, Rosemary's rescued German Spitz, came rushing out of the back and made a beeline for his owner. Little more than a ball of fluff that couldn't hurt a fly, he jumped up and down, barking fiercely.

Rosemary scooped him into her arms, where he quieted but wiggled around to lick the air near Abigail Redberry's outstretched hand. "You're quite the little guard dog, aren't you?" she cooed indulgently before rounding on Vera. "And you're back from holiday!" Abigail exclaimed. "How lovely to see you. I'm sure Rosemary is thrilled. She's missed you and Frederick terribly."

During the first couple of years Rosemary lived next to Abigail, the pair had barely spoken more than a few sentences to one another. Thrown together when Abigail's husband, a dentist, was accused of murder a few months prior, the women were now fast friends.

Even so, it was Vera who Abigail found intriguing, which came as no surprise. Anyone with eyes would find Vera intriguing, even if they weren't a fan of the theater. Given that Abigail was an avid one, she was familiar with Vera's body of work long before meeting her in the flesh. She had, ages ago, watched Vera star in a production of Othello at the outdoor stage in the nearby Regent's Park. Introducing fan to actress was a coup, one Rosemary was proud to facilitate.

While Vera's *body of work* wasn't particularly vast or even terribly illustrious, her mother's certainly had been. Everyone in England with an interest in theater knew Lorraine Blackburn's name. Her acting pedigree provided Vera with a bit of a cache, and as her star continued to rise, the consensus seemed to be she possessed enough genuine talent to live up to her mother's example. Rosemary certainly believed so, though she would admit to being entirely biased.

"Did you have a lovely time in Mallorca?" Abigail asked Vera now, her hazel eyes sparkling below a fringe of ginger bangs.

Talking about herself was one of Vera's favorite pastimes, and now that she'd a handsome husband to include in her tales, Rosemary suspected the habit would increase in both frequency and enthusiasm. Luckily, she adored both Vera and her brother, Frederick, with a fierceness only outmatched by a mother's love for her children, and so the notion merely elicited a feeling of rueful amusement.

"Simply fabulous, Abigail dear." Vera took the opening and ran with it, gushing about Mallorca, sun, and sand. "Go home, and book yourself and Martin tickets straight away!" Vera wiggled her eyebrows and winked suggestively, ignored the scandalized expression on Abigail's face, and added, "I tell you, it will do wonders for your marital relationship."

Abigail's cheeks pinked, and she stuttered, "Yes, that sounds lovely," she replied, and deftly changed the subject. "Will you be performing in a new production anytime soon?"

"Here's hoping," Vera said, crossing her fingers for luck. "I'm slated to audition for a new play that I expect will be a massive hit! Lord knows I could use a break. My last audition went horribly awry, and I fear I might not get another chance if this one also turns sour. However, I've a trick up my sleeve that's sure to impress the director."

"Certainly, it can't be as bad as all that," Abigail offered reassurance and a few more platitudes before begging off to go fix Martin's lunch. "Well, as they say, break a leg! I do hope you get the part, and once again, welcome back." With that and a nod in Rosemary's direction, she retreated to the other side of the fence.

"Is it really the role of a lifetime, Vera?" Rosemary asked when Abigail had disappeared back into her garden.

"It could be," Vera qualified, "although, couldn't they all? There are no small parts, Rosie. Only small actors. That being said, there are also *bad* parts, but I've a feeling this isn't one of them. As long as I manage to come across as authentic, I'll be fine," Vera said with conviction. It sounded, to Rosemary's ear, like an oft-repeated affirmation, but she'd rather dive into a vat of boiling acid than point out the fact. Vera could be touchy when it came to her craft.

"I'll be fine," Vera repeated, "as long as I give a better

audition than Cora Flowers."

Rosemary sucked in a breath. The last time Vera had gone up against another actress for a role, she'd ended up in a backstage fistfight that resulted in her being banned from the Globe for a considerable length of time.

"I shudder to ask," Rosemary deadpanned, her tone having no effect, whatsoever, on her friend, "but who is Cora Flowers?"

"She's new, young, and beautiful. Terrible stage name, though, don't you think? Just a bit too *on the nose* for my tastes, but she's a force to be reckoned with, all the same." Then, Vera's chest puffed up just a bit. "However, she's no match for me. I've the pedigree and the talent." Another affirmation, which counted two more than Vera typically needed.

Rosemary put her arm around her friend's shoulder. "She can't, I'm quite positive, hold a candle to you, dear. Later, if you like, we'll run lines, but for now, let's focus our efforts towards the LLV. From what I've gathered, Ivy and Esme are restless for a new mission and rather desperate to set the ball rolling."

Vera closed her eyes and let out an enormous sigh, rolled her neck, and shook her limbs in a tension-relieving gesture. "All right, I place myself in your capable hands," she said to Rosemary in a mock-serious Shakespearean accent. "I am naught but a slab of clay, ready to be molded—"

Cutting her off with a grin and another playful elbow jab to the ribs, Rosemary sent Vera back home to eat and change her clothes.

CHAPTER THREE

Once Vera was gone, Rosemary descended the stairs to the street-level space where her late husband, Andrew, once conducted his detective business. Now, the room functioned as an art studio.

Rosemary was a painter, somewhat mediocre in her own opinion, but one needn't be particularly proficient to find peace in the work.

Today, however, she pushed the canvases aside. There were no damp brushes to be found, no half-finished works of art in sight. In fact, if she took the time to contemplate such a thing, she might have felt a modicum of shame regarding the state of her supplies and the span of passing days since she'd last put paint to canvas.

Eventually, Rosemary knew she would return to her passion. She planned to dispense with the sneaking around and return to her normal life just as soon as she got to the bottom of the reason for these clandestine visits to the basement office. What Rosemary most longed for was freedom from the looming threat that hung, like a shadow, over her head for the last several months.

To that end, Rosemary pulled a pair of rolling easels out of the way, spun first one and then the other to face front. She tugged off their fabric covers to reveal not summer landscapes or even a customary bowl of fruit, but instead a chalkboard covered in delicate, detailed print and a corkboard displaying several newspaper articles and a dozen or so photographs.

As always, the photograph pinned to the board's center drew her eye first. She studied the image of a man with wild ebony hair and even wilder eyes before moving on to the two charcoal sketches tacked up beside it. Drawings of Rosemary herself done in such intricate detail she couldn't help admire the quality of the work despite the chill they sent up her spine.

Her face being known to the artist would have been concerning enough had Garrison Black simply been a mass murderer. That he was currently on the loose and evading capture after a daring escape didn't help matters at all. Black's apparent fixation compelled him to draw both sketches and leave them on her doorstep, marking her as his next victim.

Black truly was a monster in human form, and his sights were set on her. Dread mixed with morbid curiosity propelled her to dig into the case, even knowing she did so against Max's wishes as well as those of her close circle of family and friends.

In point of fact, it was only the one sketch Max and the lot worried over—because it was the only one any of them knew existed. The second, a drawing of Rosemary laid out in a coffin, a serene expression across her cold, dead face, had arrived only days before, and she'd been reluctant to turn it over to the police. Given that Max *was* the police, Rosemary was taking a serious risk in keeping its existence to herself.

It was all rather tiring, and the moment that second sketch came to light, Rosemary knew she could say goodbye to the last of her independence. Even now, they'd be quite happy to put her in a velvet-lined box and put her on a high shelf where no harm could come to her. This was not how Rosemary wanted to live her life.

If only there were a way to use sleuthing skills to help find and capture Garrison Black, but so far, he'd managed to keep to the shadows and outsmart even the police. In his capacity as chief inspector, Max kept his nose to the grindstone as he worked the case but expressed that Rosemary was to keep hers safely out of it in no uncertain terms Everyone from her mother to her butler had heartily agreed with the ban. Hence, the subterfuge to which she was forced to resort.

While not quite as free-thinking (or free-speaking) as Vera, Rosemary considered herself a contemporary woman, and she firmly believed in her right to do as she pleased. After all, it was she who sat slated as Black's next target; her exploits which had caught his attention; her face so perfectly captured in charcoal. The knowledge made her blood run cold. But given Black's fascination with her, It only stood to reason she might be the key to outsmarting him. At the very least, she ought to be able to study the case without interference.

Furthermore, she *had* solved several murders already, hadn't she? And it was she who stood to lose the most if Black wasn't thwarted soon. Rosemary sighed with exasperation but pushed the emotion from her mind and spent a few long moments staring at the boards, pondering.

Without the first clue where to look, finding Black quickly or by sheer chance was about as likely as finding a needle in a haystack. No, he was smarter than that and, as far as Rosemary could tell, driven by an entirely different need than most murderers.

What no one wanted to say, and what Rosemary knew in her bones was the best way to find him was to let him find her and then catch him in the act of attempting murder. Given his history, the odds he'd manage to pull it off—even if Max agreed to let her become bait—were too strong for her to seriously consider that investigative route.

It wasn't money or revenge that caused Black to stalk

and torment his victims, brutally killing them in their own homes, and it certainly wasn't love. No, Rosemary believed Garrison Black killed because he couldn't *not* kill, because he felt a compulsion to do so. She also believed his dark urges had something to do with his mother, that his upbringing had tainted his view of the fairer sex and twisted his relationships ever since.

Rosemary hadn't come to this conclusion based solely on a hunch or even entirely on her own. She'd studied stacks of files dedicated to the case. Files she wasn't supposed to have access to, and files that could land her in a heap of trouble with her inspector beau if found in her possession.

Mostly due to Rosemary's recent loss but also out of respect for Max's relationship with her late husband, they were taking their romance at a snail's pace. He and Andrew had been best mates, and even though Max had never—at least not intentionally or consciously— thought of Rosemary as anything more than a friend until long after Andrew's death, it was a delicate situation.

No matter the state of their romance, she considered Max a trusted friend and vice versa. For the hundredth time, Rosemary wondered what he would do if he learned she'd been keeping something this big from him.

The doorbell interrupted Rosemary's pondering, and a moment later, she let out a curse. "Speak of the devil," she huffed, having recognized Max's voice when Wadsworth welcomed him through the door.

Max didn't often visit the basement office during his trips to Rosemary's townhouse, but she'd forgotten to consider what her butler might do. Her mouth settled into a thin line as she thought about the conversation she'd have with Wadsworth later, away from the prying ears of the rest of the staff. He knew good and well what she did down there, and her staying out of the case was one of the only things upon which Wadsworth and Max unequivocally agreed.

He wouldn't tell Max outright, but Rosemary wouldn't have put it past him to let the information slip some other way.

Quickly, she tucked the file into the top drawer of what had been Andrew's desk and spun the boards back into their original position. She snatched a cloth off the nearest canvas and picked up a brush just as Max entered the room.

"Hello," Rosemary greeted Max brightly—a little too brightly—and set down the paintbrush to cross the room and plant a light kiss on his cheek.

Wadsworth turned away, but not before a hint of disapproval flitted across his eyes. To his credit, he hid it well, and even if she'd been the type to reprimand her butler for such a trivial matter, she knew his concern was only for her welfare—both physical and emotional.

Wadsworth was a good egg, so she merely rolled her eyes internally and watched as his back retreated through the door.

"Hello," Max replied, a question in his voice. He looked around the room curiously, his gaze settling on the painting Rosemary had rushed to uncover. "New project?"

Rosemary covered the awkward moment as seamlessly as possible. "Not really. I painted this one a few weeks ago, but something about it's been bothering me." While not technically a lie—she'd not quite managed the precise mix of blue, green, and white for the ocean waves she'd been trying to recreate—it also wasn't exactly the truth, either.

He didn't say anything for a moment, merely peered pensively at the seascape and shrugged. "I think it's rather smart, but who am I to tell you how to do your work?"

She'd almost decided to come clean, show him her boards of Garrison Black data, and take whatever admonishment he delivered—but Max's comment struck a nerve. Rosemary had, many times, attempted to tell him how to do *his* job, so it rang like a double entendre to her ear and raised the hairs on the back of her neck to attention.

Ignoring the rhetorical question she asked, more sharply than she'd intended, "What are you doing here, anyway?"

If Max's nostrils flared slightly, Rosemary pretended not to notice.

"I was in the neighborhood and thought I'd confirm our plans for tonight. I assume your brother and Vera are still up for an evening out."

"Never have I ever heard either of them turn down a chance to drink copiously, so yes," Rosemary replied, softening somewhat at the mention of a night on the town. It only lasted a moment because Max had slightly different ideas about whether she ought to be gallivanting about London with a murderer on the loose.

Why she refused to take more precautions was something that both mystified and grated steadily on his patience. He couldn't recall—and in fact, had little desire to try—whether Andrew had, during their years of friendship, complained overmuch about his wife's independent nature.

Rosemary could have answered that question, as the answer was, in fact, a resounding yes. Andrew, much like Max, had been a proponent of women's rights, but that didn't negate a worry over his wife's safety—something she never seemed to concern herself with!

Much like Andrew, Max considered himself lucky to keep her company, and so he pasted a smile on his face and made a silent vow to protect her at all costs. "If you're certain, I'll confirm the reservation. At least

Kettner's doesn't allow riffraff. We ought to be perfectly safe."

"Of course we will be," Rosemary replied without contemplation. Taking his hands in hers, she leaned in. "There's safety in numbers, and we'll all be together. Let's not worry, and instead try to have a nice time. It's been ages since we've enjoyed a carefree evening, and Vera and Frederick are dying to tell us all about their honeymoon." Her voice had turned to a cajole, and Max softened involuntarily.

"I've already agreed, even if it is against my better judgment," he said huskily and leaned in for one sweet kiss before straightening with a sigh. "I'd best be getting back to work before my new constable gets himself into some sort of trouble." Max rolled his eyes. "He claims he's just turned twenty, but I think your four-year-old nephew, Nelly, would be a better partner. Besides, you've...things to do." Max nodded at the easel and gave Rosemary a long, lingering look.

She couldn't tell if it had to do with the kiss, with her insistence upon carrying on as if nothing were amiss, or if he somehow knew exactly what it was she was hiding behind the rolling easels.

Knowing Max, she thought, *probably all of the above.*

Chapter Four

Once Max left, Rosemary didn't have the stomach to return to her study of Garrison Black and instead went to work setting the office back to rights. As she began rolling one of the blackboards into place to tuck it away until the sight of it didn't fill her with guilt, Vera blew through the office door and caught her, fully this time, in the act.

To Rosemary's exasperation, the charcoal drawing she had kept from Max fluttered to the floor. She bent down to pick it up and then quickly tucked it inside the first folder she could grab from the desktop.

On Vera's heels came Dash, with Wadsworth following closely behind. Each time the dog jumped at Vera's skirts, Wadsworth's lip twitched in time with the beat of the vein throbbing at his temple.

"Mrs. Woolridge has returned," Wadsworth intoned formally as if introducing Vera for the first time. His eyes flicked to the blackboards, and his jaw tightened further.

Rosemary resisted the urge to blow a raspberry in his direction while Vera exclaimed, "Oh, for heaven's sake, Wadsworth! For a moment, I thought Evelyn had somehow materialized behind me like a specter roiling out of the ether! I forbid you from referring to me as *Mrs. Woolridge* ever again. It's Miss Vera, and that'll be the end of it. Mrs. Woolridge, indeed! Say, Rosie, what's all this?"

Partway through her diatribe, Vera noticed Rosemary's glance straying toward the hidden cache of evidence. The rant ended abruptly as Vera marched across the room to get a better look. She flipped the boards around and stared at the collected articles, notes, and photographs.

"I knew it! You're obsessed. One can hardly blame you, of course. If I had a mass murderer coming after me, well, I rather think I'd do the same as you. Although, what exactly is it you're trying to do, find Black's hideout or something?"

Rosemary highly doubted Garrison Black was holed up in the type of hideout Vera was likely to imagine; this wasn't Treasure Island after all, and Black wasn't Captain Flint.

"No," Rosemary said with a firm shake of her head. "Locating Black isn't my goal. I'll leave that to the police, although I suspect they won't find him either.

More likely, he'll find me first," she declared. Her voice was strong and even, but her words sent a shiver up Vera's spine. "And when he does, I intend to be ready both for a physical challenge and also a battle of the mind. Obviously, the man has been watching and studying me; well, two can play at that game, can't they?"

Vera peered at her friend, raised an eyebrow, and nodded once. "All right, Rosie. I'll help you in whatever way I can, so long as you promise me you'll be careful, and you won't go anywhere alone. Do we have an accord?" she asked cheekily as she stepped away from the evidence of Rosemary's secret obsession and sat on the chair across from the desk.

Rosemary agreed, and the matter was settled. "There's just one thing," she added. "I haven't told Max I'm still studying Black. It's not investigating, strictly, but the line I'm walking is a fine one. I'll tell him, and not only because I think it's safe to say he already knows, but please don't mention it this evening."

"Oh, Rosie, of course," Vera laughed off the request, absently picking up Dash and settling him in her arms. "I'm nothing if not well-versed in the subtle art of manipulating a conversation. Particularly manipulating conversations with men. And besides, surely we've more titillating things to discuss. In fact, I say we ban any mention of Garrison Black this evening and just try and enjoy ourselves."

Once again, Rosemary agreed. "We had better get a move on," she said with a glance at the clock. "Ivy and Esme will be thrilled to see you, Vera. Naturally, they've been dying to hear all about Mallorca, and we wouldn't want to keep them waiting. I'll go collect the tray of refreshments Gladys prepared. I tell you, that woman is a saint."

"Right so, Rosie," Vera said, removing a reluctant Dash from her lap and following her friend up the stairs and through to the dining room. There, Anna and the saintly Gladys sat polishing silver.

Anna did a double-take, dropped the piece of cutlery she'd been holding, and rushed over to gush, "Miss Vera, you've returned! Did you have a lovely time? Was it quite romantic? Surely it must have been! Ooh, Mallorca, how positively fabulous!"

Vera laughed, took Anna's hands in hers, and gave them an affectionate squeeze. "It was absolutely the most divine month of my life! I promise to tell you all about it when Rosie and I aren't running late."

Even though Rosemary was sure she'd rather have heard all about Vera and Frederick's honeymoon right then, Anna accepted the rain check with a smile. She moved to return to the table but then appeared to have second thoughts.

"Miss Rose," she said, hesitating, "I was wondering

if—if I might have the evening off?"

Even if it had been a habit of Anna's, Rosemary wouldn't have taken more than a second to consider the request. As it stood, she couldn't remember the girl ever asking for so much as an afternoon, even when she'd been suffering from a terrible toothache and would have done better to remain home in her own bed.

"Of course!" Rosemary replied, then raised a matronly eyebrow. "Might I inquire as to your plans?"

Anna blushed scarlet and shook her head, "Nothing of consequence, I'm sure," she said, sitting back down and resuming her polishing with renewed fervor.

"Darling girl, you've a rendezvous with a boy, haven't you?" Vera said, ignoring the hint entirely. "Who is he? Not that chap who threw you over last month, I hope."

Her eyes widened, and Anna stammered evasively, "No, of course not, not him. He's just…just someone I met recently. Really, nobody of consequence."

"That I highly doubt, and anyhow you certainly deserve someone of consequence, dear," Vera replied. "What are you planning to wear?"

Another blush crept into Anna's cheeks. "I've no idea!" she bemoaned, tears threatening to spill from her eyes. Across the table, Gladys's nostrils flared as she fought a battle with her own eyes to keep them from rolling skyward.

Rosemary's lip twitched. Oh, to be young and

innocent again. She vehemently wished she could return to the time in her life where the biggest concern was which dress to pair with which wrap and what hairstyle to wear for the big dance. Since she very much doubted the next car to pull up to the curb would be a time machine, Rosemary instead indulged Anna's whims and shot a rueful smile in Gladys's direction.

"I'll tell you what, dear girl," Vera said, leaning down to finger a lock of Anna's hair, "once you've finished with the silver, I want you to go to my house and pick out any dress that catches your fancy. I do recommend the powder blue one with the beading, however. It will look smashing with your complexion. While you're there, gather my things, and we'll all get ready together. I'll even do your hair up nice. This mystery date of yours isn't going to know what hit him. Of course, this does mean you'll have to reveal his identity."

Now Anna squealed with delight and flung her arms around Vera's neck. "Thank you, Miss Vera! Oh, I'm sorry, I've mussed your hair," she said, pulling away quickly.

"Never you mind. I'll fix it right up on the ride," Vera replied, amused, and winked at Anna. "So long as our Rosie doesn't drive like a maniac."

On their way out the door, Rosemary heard Gladys tell Anna she'd finish the silver herself and chuckled at the thought that two gifts had fallen into Anna's lap in quick succession.

"So, my love, what else is new?" Vera asked when they'd settled into the car. "It's been an age since we engaged in a proper chinwag!"

Rosemary thought for a moment and then answered, "Oh, there is one thing you'll be interested to know. Stella and Leonard are contemplating a trip to America."

"Really?" Vera asked, impressed. "For what purpose?"

"Leonard is one of the candidates for a professorial exchange program. If he's accepted—I gather he's a shoo-in—he'll teach architecture at a university there for a semester, and one of their professors will teach in his place at Oxford."

Gobsmacked, Vera said, "They'll stay for that long? And Stella will accompany him, with the children? Ooh, Evelyn must be positively gutted!" If she sounded overly gleeful at the thought, Rosemary decided she couldn't blame her. Her mother and Vera treated each other like family—if that family were made up of Montagues and Capulets. Sparks flew between the women no matter how hard Vera tried to please.

Not that Vera tried overmuch. She flouted most of the rules to which Evelyn clung so fiercely. Later, a brief detente ensued when Vera was poised to marry the eldest Woolridge brother, Lionel. Then, after Lionel was killed in the war, Evelyn maintained a close friendship with Vera's mother, Lorraine, but treated Vera like a piece of old luggage.

Their relationship worsened when Frederick and Vera began courting; Evelyn felt Vera had betrayed Lionel, which of course, was categorically unfair. She'd softened, eventually, and the pair had made their peace, but Rosemary suspected it was a tenuous one.

The smile on Vera's face did nothing to quell the concern.

Chapter Five

From the outside, the building where the LLV convened looked like nothing special, nothing more than an old, abandoned school building Ivy Gibson had convinced her husband to buy for a song. Members assumed Commissioner Gibson had no clue as to the goings-on; that he believed his wife to be off playing bridge or planting petunias with the garden club.

Rosemary had met Commissioner Gibson enough times to know he was no bumbling, oblivious idiot. It was far more likely, in her estimation, Ivy's husband knew exactly what his wife was up to. He'd have been a fool to try to talk her out of it and a fool the chief was not.

Upon arriving and noting the improved state of the front garden, Vera let out a low whistle and said, "Well, now, they've done a lot with the space."

"*We've* done a lot with the space," Rosemary corrected, pride evident in her tone.

Vera quickly connected the dots. This was where her friend's new obsession with gardening had been born, and Max's mother, Ariadne, had done her best to fan the flames. "Point taken," Vera said with a grin.

Inside, things looked much the same. The LLV hadn't transformed the gymnasium, which continued to function much as it always had except that now, instead of a space for children to exercise, it was a place where a ragtag group of ladies—mostly police wives—gathered to work both their bodies and their minds.

Yes, inside things looked much the same, but they certainly didn't *feel* the way they had only a few short weeks before. As a group, though in no small part due to Rosemary's brush with Garrison Black, the ladies had decided to ramp up their efforts on all fronts.

"Some of us aren't satisfied to merely improve ourselves," Rosemary explained. "We'd like to make the world—or at least London—a better place. To play some role, however small, in the betterment of others. Today we'll be taking suggestions for how to do so."

Vera snorted and said so only Rosemary could hear, "I'm sure you've already devised a master plan and will, in short order, convince this lot to follow your lead."

"Oh, no," Rosemary disagreed, holding up her hands and waving away the notion. "I've every intention of going along with whatever Ivy and Esme choose. They started the group, so they ought to be the ones who decide what direction it will take moving forward. I am content to follow."

Vera shrugged but followed Rosemary inside. Several smiling women waved at her. One of the newer recruits, an obvious bottle-blond by the name of Hadley Walsh, rushed over to say hello.

Rosemary rolled her eyes. She didn't much care for Hadley; the girl—for she wasn't much more than one— was far too perky for Rosemary's liking and, unfortunately, seemed to crave her attention more than anyone else's in the group.

"Pleased to meet you," Hadley said. "Any friend of Rosemary's, as they say." Vera thought Hadley might move on then, but Rosemary knew better. She held back a smirk as the girl chattered. "We're so lucky to have a real detective in our midst! One who has actually solved a few murders, even. It's incredible, truly, a real coup. I'm so pleased my dear friend, Maddy—see the willowy brunette over there?—brought me along."

Hadley shivered dramatically. "I felt quite certain I was to be Garrison Black's next victim. I mean, look at me, blond hair and blue eyes—I'm just his type, *and* I live right near where Arabelle Grey was attacked.

"Well," Hadley qualified, "Arabelle's flat was in Mayfair, quite close to me, as the crow flies."

Arabelle Grey had almost been murdered several months prior. A wealthy heiress, she'd sailed off to

America—and taken one of Max's constables with her—after escaping Black's clutches. Her attack and subsequent exodus from England had been in all the papers.

"Maddy suggested I come to group one day," Hadley continued to prattle on. "You know, get fit, learn to defend myself. Why, she said she even learned how to fire a gun while she was here! I do hope we'll do that again soon."

Ivy Gibson spotted Rosemary and Vera, and seeing them being harangued by the eager Hadley, mercifully called the meeting to order. Everyone took a seat at a long table and looked towards where Ivy stood next to a seated Esme Prescott, the group's second in command.

"Well, talk with you both later, and again, lovely to meet you, Vera," Hadley finished up, beamed at Rosemary, and then went to settle herself next to her friend.

"I think she's still talking," Vera said when Hadley was out of earshot. "I bet she talks to herself even when she's alone."

Rosemary thought perhaps Vera was correct.

"Come now, everyone. We've an important task to complete today," Ivy boomed. She commanded a room with just as much authority as her husband commanded his department. "Last week, we agreed to consider our options and return to the group with suggestions for a way to serve our community. Who would like to go first?"

Several eager hands shot into the air, a few of them going so far as to wave around excitedly.

"Yes, Minerva," Esme motioned to a pretty, robust redhead with a turned-up nose. "What do you propose?"

Minerva, evidently, didn't relish speaking out loud because her cheeks pinked slightly as she glanced nervously around and appeared to have second thoughts. "Well," she said doubtfully, "there's always the widows, isn't there? We could join the pension efforts or volunteer at one of the shelters."

"Not bad," Ivy said, turning to the chalkboard that two of the other ladies had quickly rolled into place at the head of the table. She began a list and added Minerva's suggestion. "Anyone else?"

The oldest member of the group, a surprisingly spry septuagenarian whose husband had been Commissioner just before Ivy's, stood and said, "I recommend we fight against styles of clothing the young girls are wearing. Short skirts and icepick heels, indeed!"

"Mrs. Higgins!" Vera blurted, having taken the comment as a personal attack. "Why would you want us to launch a crusade against fashion? Who would that possibly help?"

Mrs. Higgins looked Vera up and down and, with a disapproving glower, replied, "These girls today dress like streetwalkers and then find themselves in trouble, no husbands to speak of. Perhaps if they held themselves to a higher standard, we wouldn't have so many bastard children running 'round London!"

Rosemary blanched, and Vera fired back, "I propose we volunteer at one of the birth control clinics," countering Mrs. Higgins' comment in a game of tit-for-tat. She looked as though she might leap across the table and throttle the old lady with her bare hands.

Ivy Gibson mercifully intervened again. She was nothing if not a master at the art of redirection. "Perhaps we ought to stay away from some of the more controversial topics and focus instead on something we *all* agree is an important cause. I suppose the war widows would do smartly, or we could join the parks and gardens cause. Heaven knows there are neighborhoods in London that could benefit from further beautification efforts."

Planting flowers wasn't precisely what Rosemary had in mind, and it seemed she wasn't the only one.

"How about the ex-servicemen?" Hadley Walsh piped up without further explanation.

"What about them?" Ivy asked.

Hadley stood and asked, "Hasn't anyone been following the story of the homeless ex-servicemen? The Tommies fought for England, and now, so very many of them are unfit to return to their previous jobs. The

British Legion, of course, is trying, but they're overwhelmed and understaffed. Our heroes are languishing on the streets of London—and I don't mean the West End."

It certainly sounded like a worthy cause to Rosemary, and it was clear from the expression on both Ivy's and Esme's faces that they felt the same.

"What exactly are you proposing?" Someone asked.

With a shrug, Hadley passed the buck. "What else? Volunteer at one of the shelters, like Minerva suggested. Isn't that what we ladies do?"

The room vibrated with interested chatter, and it seemed as though the group had found a direction in which to focus their efforts. Eventually, it was decided that a fact-finding mission would commence the following week in the interest of aiding England's brave soldiers.

"I don't much fancy venturing into the East End without a specific destination," Mrs. Higgins said when talk of visiting the disreputable part of London began to form into a concrete plan.

"I'll make some inquiries first," Ivy promised. "Get the lay of the land, so to speak. If these shelters are understaffed, they ought to be thrilled to receive our assistance. We'll be perfectly safe. Of course, we are a volunteer group; if you feel uncomfortable, you're under no obligation to attend." It was clear from Ivy's tone she would prefer Mrs. Higgins *did* beg off. "Furthermore, it's not as though we'll be traipsing around in the middle of the night. It will be afternoon, and there's safety in numbers."

It was nearly the same argument Rosemary had made in defense of visiting Kettner's that evening. If any of the other women were skeptical, Ivy's confidence was all it took to either convince them otherwise or discourage further disagreement.

The moment Ivy officially dismissed the meeting, Esme hurried over. "Vera, how lovely to see you," she said, briefly clasping Vera's hands in her own dainty ones and exchanging pleasantries. The pair discussed Mallorca for a long few moments before Ivy sidled over, accompanied by the chattering Hadley.

A repeat of the Mallorca conversation ensued, and then Ivy asked Vera a question that caused Rosemary to groan internally. Ivy was, for more reasons than one, the matriarch of the group. Older than most of the ladies by a couple of decades, she was still a formidable force of a woman and though by no means stodgy, a bit old-fashioned when it came to certain matters.

Before long, as Rosemary had expected, Vera's voice rose, her tone cold enough to chill a cocktail glass. "There's more to life than having children."

Esme blanched and dropped her gaze to inspect the floor while color returned to redden her cheeks.

Rosemary's heart went out to Esme, and a sympathetic expression crossed her face. Noticing the silent exchange, Vera made a startling discovery about her friend.

For the first time, she realized Rosemary and Esme shared certain similarities and were, in some respects, far more alike than were Rosemary and herself. Both women had been widowed, and though Vera and Lionel were engaged when he died, they were naught more than children at the time. A pang of something close to jealousy pierced her heart even though she knew it was ridiculous.

Hadley, who hadn't been around long enough to fully grasp the dynamics of the group, looked between Ivy and Vera with avid curiosity. Her eyes twinkled expectantly, but if she was hoping for a catfight, she would be sorely disappointed.

"My apologies," Ivy said breezily, not easily ruffled. "I forget you modern young ladies have other priorities these days." Ivy's comment brought Vera back around to the conversation at hand, but for once, out of respect for Rosemary, she kept her opinion to herself.

The mood somewhat deflated, Rosemary prepared to leave, but halfway to the exit, Esme stopped her. In her hand, she held a small, leather-bound notebook, the sight of which quickened Rosemary's heartbeat.

The Garrison Black murder case had spanned a

decade, beginning with his first set of murders: three flaxen-haired women Black stalked and tormented. He entered their homes, lay in wait, and then struck when least expected, brutally beating and eventually shooting each one through her heart.

Proof he felt some sick sense of pride in his crimes, Black would leave a calling card at each of the scenes—an actual card with a drawing of a shriveled black heart shape on the back. It was enough to give every blond woman in the city a good scare.

At the time of his death, Esme's late husband, Sergeant Nathaniel Prescott, had been the lead investigator in the case. As a young constable, he had helped investigate the scene of Black's first murder. What he saw there shook him to his core. Prescott vowed to see justice served, and for ten years, he relentlessly studied and tracked, making Black's capture his singular goal.

Unfortunately, Prescott had only briefly seen that goal realized. Black somehow managed to escape from jail, and then Prescott was murdered—not by Black himself, but due to his actions.

A thorough investigator, and save for one bad call—a call that had, ultimately, cost him his life—Prescott had been an exemplary officer. His accolades alone would have told Rosemary that, but she'd been honored with the opportunity to acquaint herself with the man on a more personal level, posthumously, through his notes and journals. That honor was all thanks to his wife, Esme, who had vowed, months prior, to assist Rosemary with the Black case in any way she could.

Now, Esme took a furtive look around. Only Hadley Walsh's hawk-like eyes were trained in their direction, but she was well out of earshot. Even so, Esme lowered her voice before explaining, "I found this in a box of Nate's things, and I thought you might like to take a look at it. It's dated around the time of the second trio of murders."

"Thank you," Rosemary said, stowing the journal in her handbag. "I know it's asking a lot, but—"

Esme cut her off. "It's nothing. If it was me he was threatening, I wouldn't sleep until he was hanging from the gallows."

Chapter Six

Anna did indeed choose the blue dress that Vera had suggested for her. However, she admitted to having fondled a particularly luxurious slinky red velvet number for quite a long moment before finalizing her choice. As she'd promised to do, Vera curled Anna's hair into a casual yet fetching updo with a single finger curl at her right temple.

When asked for an opinion, Rosemary stepped back to survey Vera's work, nodding in approval. "Just enough, I think. He'll be left wondering why he can't stop staring at you all evening," she added with a wink that did little to improve Anna's spirits.

The poor girl looked scared nearly to death. "Would you like a nip of brandy before you head out?" Rosemary asked. "It might calm your nerves."

A quick shake of Anna's head and a widening of her eyes answered the question. "That would only make it worse." She'd still refused to reveal the identity of her date, and for once, even Vera had the sense not to press too hard. They'd find out in due course and if it somehow made Anna feel better to keep her secret, so be it.

The idea had been to gussy the girl up and send her on her way at half-past seven when her date was slated to arrive. This would give Rosemary and Vera just enough time to assess the boy and then shoo the pair of them out the door before Max and Frederick arrived at eight o'clock.

By a quarter-to-eight, Anna had gone from frantically pacing to slumped on the parlor sofa, her face plastered with the dejected expression most often worn by the recently thrown-over.

"Perhaps he got the time wrong," Vera suggested hopefully with a wide-eyed grimace only Rosemary could see.

"Or, perhaps he's stuck at work," Rosemary supplied.

Vera tried another tack when neither suggestion provided any comfort for poor Anna. "He might well have gotten lost. Are you positive you gave him accurate directions?"

"That can't be it—" Anna's denial was interrupted by the sound of the doorbell ringing, and a lovely, hopeful smile lit her face for a moment before Frederick's voice echoed through the entrance hall. As charming as Anna might find Rosemary's brother, his arrival was, for once, less than welcome.

"Ahh, Wadsworth, good to see you, old chap. No worries, no worries, I've got the door," Frederick boomed, "I can see myself inside, though why my dear sister hasn't greeted me personally after I've been away for weeks is a mystery!"

Rosemary didn't rush to greet Frederick, but she did take a few steps towards the door and met him with a smile. She let him wrap his arms around her and lift her off the floor; there was no talking Freddie out of his customary greeting.

When he finally deposited her back onto her feet with an indulgent smile, Rosemary noticed Frederick wasn't alone. Accompanied by his new constable, a wiry young lad named Morris Clayton, Max trailed behind Frederick.

She opened her mouth to ask what he was doing there but shut it quickly as the realization dawned on her: Constable Clayton was Anna's escort for the evening, and by the looks of it, Max was in the process of drawing the same conclusion. He frowned at Rosemary, and when she gave him a subtle nod, flicked a glance at the young couple. Anna's face pinked, as did the constable's. *The poor things*, Rosemary thought, *haven't the least idea how to proceed with their courtship.*

"S—Sorry to intrude," the constable stuttered, directing his comment towards Rosemary but seeming to struggle with how to properly address her. "I'm afraid I'm rather late." He glanced at Max nervously but avoided Anna's gaze, obviously embarrassed.

Graciously, Max took the blame, "It's my fault, that. I've made him late while somehow managing to arrive early. Two faux pas in one shot; that's rather impressive in its own right, wouldn't you say, Fred?"

"In reputable company, yes, quite," Frederick retorted, grinning, and then added, "though not a personal best if I do say so myself!"

The comment only seemed to further puzzle the young Mr. Clayton, who wasn't the brightest candle in the chandelier as far as Rosemary could tell.

Still, Anna appeared smitten. From beneath lowered lashes, she kept her eyes trained on the constable's face. Rosemary didn't think the girl had taken a full breath since he'd walked into the parlor.

Not that Rosemary could blame her; Morris Clayton looked exactly like a respectable young woman's dream: fresh-faced with wide, innocent eyes above a crooked, somewhat mischievous smile. His expression suggested his companion could expect an evening of excitement coupled with a reassurance of safety that the title of constable only served to complement.

However, in Rosemary's opinion, the illusion of competency was all on the surface, and not because she thought he'd any deep, dark secrets to keep. No, it was simply that the boy hadn't enough sense to fill a thimble with. She had, the previous week, watched him tie his shoelaces together twice in a row before he realized what he'd done. Deceptive was his appearance, but unintentionally and harmlessly so.

"Well, you'd best be off," Rosemary took mercy on both Anna and poor Mr. Clayton and excused them for their evening out.

Once they'd gone, Max turned to her and apologized again. When Rosemary waved off the sentiment, Max said, "Take my word for it. If he hangs around for any length of time, you'll understand why I'm sorry."

"Oh, don't be so dramatic, Max," Vera said with a wave, pretending not to realize the irony of those words exiting her mouth. "He's a harmless boy, and he'd be lucky to land a girl like Anna."

Max pressed his lips together and squinted. "Indeed he would, and yes, perhaps he's harmless, but he's also hapless and one of the most frustratingly daft young men I've ever met. If he makes it through training before I've throttled him with my bare hands, it will be a miracle."

***

It hardly felt as though she and Max had been courting long enough to establish a favorite restaurant. Nevertheless, Kettner's fit the bill. The London institution's champagne room reeked of sophistication, with its gleaming circular bar and twinkling chandeliers.

The food wasn't bad, either, and Rosemary had been dreaming about their scrummy roasted quail for weeks. Now that all the people she cared about were back in England safe and sound, she felt as though a weight had been lifted from her shoulders. This would be an evening like any other evening, a soothing balm for Rosemary's tattered nerves.

Tonight, she vowed, she'd think no more about Garrison Black and focus only on how wonderful it felt to be free from the crushing worry, even if only for a few hours. Being a woman who lived up to her word, that's exactly what Rosemary did. It wasn't even a terribly difficult task in the jovial wake of Vera and Frederick's return.

"So, Vera, are you planning on—" Max began once they'd ordered and tucked into cocktails, only to be cut off by an exasperated outburst.

"Don't even think about finishing that sentence, Max Whittington. I don't care if you're an officer of the law or not. I'll be forced to cause you bodily harm!" Vera warned.

Max's eyebrows shot towards his hairline, and he glanced between Rosemary and Frederick for help, the former averting his gaze with a barely-concealed grin and the latter entirely unconcerned.

"What hornet's nest did I inadvertently poke a stick into?" Max asked, bewildered. "I merely wondered if you would be appearing in any productions this theater season."

Vera's eyes widened, and she let out a peal of silvery laughter. "Oh! I suppose I may have overreacted. You see, I thought you were asking about whether Freddie and I are planning on having children right away. It would make the dozenth time I'd heard the same question today!"

"Mother's been thoroughly taxing, I'm afraid, though why either of you thought she would behave any differently is a mystery," Rosemary piped up, giddy from the banter she'd been missing for weeks and from the effects of her first, quickly gulped G&T.

"Rosie, we promised to talk only of pleasant topics this evening, so if we could commence with the Evelyn conversation, I would greatly appreciate it," Vera implored and then changed the subject. "I *am* auditioning for a new play, Max, as a matter of fact. It's a mystery set in a hotel, and I'd play the unlikely American lady sleuth who solves the case! Isn't it brilliant?" Vera gushed. "Better yet, I've a real-life lady detective to emulate. Rosie will be my muse!"

It was the first Rosemary had heard of Vera's plans, and she nearly choked on her cocktail when her head whipped involuntarily in her friend's direction. "You must be putting me on," she said with a raised brow.

"Not in the slightest, darlin'," Vera replied with a perfectly straight face—a commendable task considering she spoke with an American accent, in a dialect Rosemary recognized as hailing from the southern part of the country. A southern drawl, she believed they called it. While lilting and somewhat pleasant in its own way, the accent fell hard on Rosemary's ear.

"Oh, how glorious! We've two chances to be thoroughly entertained—the play itself and the preparation for it—assuming Rosemary doesn't throttle my wife before opening night!" Frederick appeared positively gleeful at the prospect, his wide grin wiping the smile off his sister's face. Quickly, before he noticed, she rearranged her expression into one of delight.

"I'll be happy to help you hone your craft, Vera darling, in any way I can." Rosemary would rather sit through a three-hour lecture on the rules of cricket than let Frederick know how little she relished the thought of Vera following her around playing the mirror game for the foreseeable future. She'd rather sit through a *five*-hour lecture on the rules of cricket than *allow* Vera to follow her around, but sibling rivalry often trumps reason.

Vera pierced Frederick with a glare that could have stripped paint off a wall but had little effect on his mood.

He merely grinned wider and raised an eyebrow at Rosemary in challenge. He could see right through her, of course, and she knew it.

"How about we put a little money on the line?" Frederick asked mischievously. "What do you say, Rosie? I predict you'll snap before the play even opens."

Rosemary's nostrils flared once, and she raised an eyebrow before replying evenly. "Whatever amount you're suggesting, double it."

Rather than appear concerned, Frederick merely smiled wider and reached across the table to shake his sister's hand. "Deal."

"Thank you, Rose," Vera said, turning from Frederick with her nose in the air. "It seems my husband fancies sleeping in the guest bedroom his first night in our new home."

Frederick sat up straight in his chair. "You heard it with your own ears, ladies and gents! Barely back from our honeymoon, and already she's banishing me to sleep alone. They weren't kidding when they said romance is the first thing to go. I tell you, why I ever thought it was a good idea to shackle myself to a dame, I'll never know!"

"Oh, that's a blatant lie, Frederick Woolridge," Vera said, smiling fondly in his direction now.

Rosemary's eyes met Max's in a smile that dazzled. He felt quite lucky to be included in the inside jokes and lighthearted teasing that continued throughout the rest of the meal. When dinner was finished, and the check paid, the foursome exited to the street in search of a taxi, full near to bursting with delicious food, excellent drink, and pleasant feelings.

Finding no cars waiting, they headed off at a lively walk in the general direction of the London neighborhood Vera and Frederick now shared with Rosemary. The conversation continued as the two couples wove their way through the streets until suddenly Frederick, who was in the lead, did a double-take on his way past a darkened alley and stopped short, stiffening.

The temperature seemed to drop by several degrees, and Vera reached out instinctively to clutch Rosemary's arm. Rosemary peered around her brother's tensed figure and stifled a gasp. There, no more than ten feet away, stood a young woman, the terrified expression on her face illuminated in a dim shaft of moonlight.

A man faced her, turned away from the entrance to the alley, his arm raised high above his head. In his hand, a knife glistening threateningly. His victim didn't make a sound, but her gaze shifted, alerting her attacker to the presence of witnesses.

He spun, and for one long, terrible moment, his gaze shifted from the four people staring at him to the weapon in his grasp.

CHAPTER SEVEN

It took Rosemary a moment longer than it ought to have to comprehend the situation playing out at the other end of the alley. In all fairness, she usually happened upon crime scenes after the fact as opposed to in the middle, so she cut herself some slack.

Fortunately, neither Frederick nor Max experienced the same moment of hesitation, and the pair of them simultaneously sprang into action and lunged at the attacker. Rosemary watched it all play out in slow motion; watched the wicked tip of the knife turn towards Frederick, watched the man's eyes widen during the split second before impact, and then close tightly as he tumbled to the ground beneath the combined weight of those who'd foiled his dastardly plan.

Steel clattered on stone, tinkled as the knife skittered away.

"Oof," Frederick stated clearly as an elbow landed in the hollow below his ribs.

"Freddie!" Vera shouted. The gloom made it impossible to tell if the knife had fallen before or after making contact with either of the heroic men.

The cowering victim let out a shriek that Rosemary felt utterly certain could have shattered glass, and it only increased in intensity when her attacker began to struggle against Frederick's grasp. "You're just making it worse for yourself, you know," Frederick said to the man in a tone that might have sounded amused to the casual ear but carried a distinct edge those who knew him well would instantly recognize. Rosemary echoed Vera's sigh of relief, then uttered a second when Freddie and Max hauled the attacker to his feet, somewhat more roughly than was necessary, not that anyone would blame them under the circumstances. Neither man appeared to be injured.

Rosemary pulled the frightened woman away from the fray, tucked an arm around her for protection while the man continued to struggle, and then spat in Frederick's direction. The manhandling suddenly seemed entirely justified.

"Enough," Max bellowed authoritatively. "Your name?"

The beady-eyed man clamped his lips shut.

"Doesn't matter. I'm placing you under arrest. "

"You can't arrest me," the unnamed man flicked his head to clear a shock of dirty hair from falling into his face. He protested, still trying to break free despite being pinned by Frederick's strong arms. "You've no authority!"

Max opened his mouth to explain that he did, in fact, possess such authority, but Frederick beat him to the punch. "That's where you're wrong, mate!" He appeared to be thoroughly enjoying himself, so much so he hadn't noticed the vein in Max's temple or the flare of his nostrils. "He's a CI, and you're in for it now!"

"Let's go," Max said, shooting Frederick a quelling look and turning back in the direction from whence they'd come. "Are you all right, Miss?" he asked the woman.

"Y—Yes," she stammered, leaning on Rosemary and Vera with palpable relief. "I think so. Thank you. He kept demanding more money, but I'd already given him everything I had. I don't know what I might have done if you...if you hadn't come along." She swallowed hard, the severity of her predicament sinking in. "I think I'd be dead."

Frederick drew himself up to his full height and replied, "Just doing our civic duty, Madam." He spoke for the entire group and earned another pinched frown from Max.

An hour later, after the on-duty constable had arrived, Max gave terse instructions, organizing an arrest and arranging for the victim to make an official statement.

Finally, as the man was being carted away, Frederick opened his mouth to make one more flip remark.

"Perhaps I ought to have joined the ranks, huh, Max? I think I did pretty well as your right hand, all things considered. Except maybe we ought to have a code word, so next time we both don't lunge at the same moment."

Excited beyond measure, Freddie snapped his fingers. "What do you think about tally-ho?" Before Max had time to respond, Freddie offered more suggestions. "Or biffer. Wouldn't that be spiffing?"

"You're speaking nonsense." Rosemary put a hand on his arm to get him to stop.

"I'm speaking cricket." Freddie fairly danced in place. "But I take your point. It lacks a certain something." Rapid-fire, he tried a few more, including combinations, each more ridiculous than the last. "Spiffing biffer. Tally biffer. Googly."

"Fits you." Freddie registered the comment but not the dry manner of his wife's delivery.

Some people react oddly to charged situations. Maybe, Rosemary thought, Freddie had lost control of his tongue for that reason.

"Biffing ho."

"Freddie!" Rosemary tried to get him to stop.

"Googly ho. By Jove, I think it's winning."

Max finally snapped. "The codeword is chief

inspector! Meaning I'm *always* the one to lunge. You should have hung back with your sister and your wife. I'm a trained professional, and you are, at best, an amateur, and at worst, a vigilante who put his companions in mortal danger!"

Frederick appeared unruffled by Max's exclamation, which was one of his worst and best qualities all rolled into one. "You're quite all right, aren't you, darling?" This he directed at Vera, who nodded exasperatedly. She happened to agree with Max and would have preferred her husband to remain safely out of harm's way.

"We're both perfectly fine," Rosemary answered for herself and Vera, "but perhaps we ought to have you checked to see if you've suffered a recent head injury. What were you thinking, Freddie?"

She didn't expect him to feel any sort of remorse or even understand that he'd put himself in danger and Max in a difficult position. In some ways, her brother could be quite exasperating, and this was one of those times when Rosemary felt a strong desire to thoroughly throttle him.

"Oh, Rosie, you worry far too much. So do the lot of you, for that matter. A man needs a bit of excitement now and then. Keeps the blood running warm, don't you know?" Frederick, being Frederick, merely laughed off his sister's admonishment, and Rosemary found herself unable to summon the strength to continue the argument.

It appeared Max felt the same way because he let the subject drop even though Rosemary could tell he was still annoyed by the way he barely spoke during the taxi ride back home. She found herself hoping Vera and Frederick would continue on to their new house; expected the pair of them to commence with their first evening alone together there, but Frederick helped Vera from the car in front of Rosemary's and followed her and Max up the steps.

"I think I fancy a stiff drink after that experience," Frederick said by way of explanation. "Why don't we break out the good stuff, Rosie. I know you're hiding a bottle of expensive cognac in the back of your drinks cupboard."

It was true. Rosemary had been saving the bottle for a special occasion, and for some reason, she felt loathe to crack it open now, especially when she really wanted everyone to go home and leave her in peace.

How had it all gone so wrong so quickly? One moment, they'd been gallivanting about as though they hadn't a care in the world, and the next, she was watching her brother and her beau take down a crazed mugger wielding a deadly weapon.

Now, Rosemary felt a headache coming on and pinched the bridge of her nose before answering. A subtle nod from Vera, who looked like she, too, was about to drop, sealed Rosemary's decision. "Not tonight,

Freddie, please. It's been rather a long day, and I'm feeling quite tired."

Frederick's eyes narrowed, his gaze flicked to Max, who appeared poised to follow his sister inside, but he evidently decided to keep his thoughts to himself and instead graciously accepted Rosemary's statement.

"Until tomorrow then, sister dear," he said, depositing a quick peck on her cheek. "It's good to be home."

Vera heartily agreed with the sentiment and said her goodbyes. The newlyweds tottered off down the street, and when they'd turned the corner at the far end, Rosemary finally opened the door and allowed Max to usher her inside.

Chapter Eight

"I'd better let you get some rest," Max said. "It's late, and I suspect Wadsworth would like to retire for the evening." The butler had refrained from opening the door during their sojourn on the steps, but it was clear he'd been waiting up for his mistress's party to return.

Now, he maintained an impassive expression. It was his job to be at Rosemary's beck and call, to keep his personal desires and thoughts to himself, and Wadsworth took pride in a job well done.

"Not yet," Rosemary said. "I wasn't entirely truthful with Frederick; I'd like a brandy if you'd care to stay and have a drink with me."

It was all the invitation Max required, but something near the telephone desk caught his eye as he passed by on the way to the parlor.

"What's that?" he asked, his voice having turned cold—downright frosty in fact. Rosemary feared she knew exactly what he was talking about but pretended not to.

"What's what?" she asked, attempting to feign ignorance and failing miserably.

Max turned to face her, the clearly labeled folder from her Garrison Black research in his hands. She knew if he opened it, he would find the charcoal drawing she'd withheld, and her heart hurt in anticipation of the deepening pain he'd feel at her betrayal. He would see the obvious and irrefutable fact that she had spent weeks deceiving him and, worse, had willingly withheld evidence in an ongoing police investigation.

In short, the last thing in the world Rosemary wanted was for Max to open that folder, but there was no stopping him now—now that he'd seen the emotions play across her face. He might not be able to read her mind, but he could certainly read her expression and what she saw reflected in his eyes made her heart constrict painfully.

She stood frozen for a long moment. This wasn't how Max was supposed to find out about her exploits. How the folder had ended up on the telephone table, she couldn't be certain. Last she knew, she'd left it in the basement office, but she had a sneaking suspicion Wadsworth was responsible.

She looked for the probable culprit but discovered he'd disappeared, probably gone to his quarters, and just in the nick of time, too. Rosemary would deal with him later, and though she wouldn't terminate his employment—Wadsworth had always been far more than just a butler—he was due for a tongue lashing.

"It's—it's not as bad as it looks," she stammered, unsure if she was trying to convince Max or herself.

"I think I ought to be the one to make that determination, don't you?" he replied icily before opening the folder and scanning the page. His eyes widened and flicked to her stricken face. "What is this, Rosemary?"

Rosemary wanted to lie, wished briefly that a suitable one would come to mind. She would have done anything at that moment to take back what she'd done. Honesty was, Max had told her at the start of their courtship, paramount in a relationship. He'd made no bones about his expectations, and she had assured him—with absolute certainty at the time—that she'd never see fit to break his trust.

Perhaps she even could have come up with something believable, or at least a spin that might put her in a marginally better light, but Rosemary was, under normal circumstances, an upstanding and honest woman. Given the events of the evening, she certainly didn't have it in her to keep up the charade any longer. "It's a second threat," she said finally, "from Garrison Black."

"It's evidence, is what it is," Max retorted. "Evidence that Garrison Black is still stalking you, still watching your house, and still wanting you dead. Evidence you should have handed over to me immediately. You just can't help yourself, can you?" he spat. "When did this arrive, Rosemary? How long have you been keeping it a secret?"

Suddenly, Rosemary felt light-headed and worried she might swoon like a damsel. If she could have made an escape to the parlor for the aforementioned brandy, she would have, but both she and Max remained rooted to the floor.

"The drawing only arrived a couple of days ago," Rosemary said slowly, "but I've been researching Garrison Black since the beginning." She drew herself up tall and looked Max square in the eyes. "I won't apologize for that part. It's me in his sights; me he wants to add to his list of victims. You can't expect me to simply carry on as though I've not a worry in the world."

Max took a deep breath. It was a long moment before he replied. "And you can't expect me to ignore the gross negligence of withholding evidence in a murder case. I'm the chief inspector, Rosemary, for chrissake!"

She'd never heard Max curse before or seen his eyes as stormy as they were when they met hers. For the second time that night, adrenaline coursed through his veins.

"That's why I didn't tell you! I didn't want to overstep

my bounds and put you in a compromising position," Rosemary said defensively, realizing that they were the wrong ones as soon as the words left her lips.

"I'm already *in* a compromising position, Rose, and you know that to be true! You've only made it worse by keeping this from me. I've known about the research; you aren't as sneaky as you believe yourself to be."

The statement came out more harshly than he'd intended, and Max saw Rosemary's face fall but couldn't stop the words from pouring out of his mouth no matter how hard he tried.

"That, I can live with, although since I abhor secrets and dishonesty, I'd prefer it out in the open. *This* is entirely different." He indicated the drawing. "When will you learn to leave things to the professionals?"

Rosemary did, of course, feel contrite, but something else inside her suddenly flared with indignation. She, too, couldn't seem to stop her emotions from see-sawing. "When will you learn it's not in my nature to sit idly by?" she retorted. "And when, precisely, did you turn into the type of man who would want me to do so?"

"When I realized I love you, Rose!" Max thundered. "When I realized I'd rather die myself than let you become Garrison Black's next victim! But if it's always going to be like this—if you're always going to hold me at arm's length and do whatever you please no matter the consequences, perhaps none of what I feel matters anyway."

Max threw the folder back onto the telephone table and stormed past Rosemary. His eyes met hers briefly, and what she saw in them made it impossible for her to speak another word.

The slamming of the door felt like an ending, but Rosemary fought back the tears and steeled herself against the pain. She'd been through worse, lord knew, and was determined that this time, she would not crumble into despair. Instead, she squared her shoulders, bolted the door, and ascended the stairs to her bedroom.

Rosemary washed and readied herself for bed, focusing on the tasks in front of her while attempting, unsuccessfully, to shut out the memory of what had just transpired.

It had been quite a while since she had felt the need to down a sleeping draught before bed; months since grief had been so debilitating, she could scarcely close her eyes without her imagination running wild with depressing thoughts. But that night, after her first-ever real fight with Max, Rosemary gulped the brew gratefully and laid her head on her pillow, hoping sleep would arrive swiftly and pull her into the dreamless, inky black. Hoping that soon, she wouldn't have to hear Max's words echoing through her mind.

Once she was in bed, though, she couldn't stop the fight—for it had been more than a mere argument—

from replaying over and over through her thoughts on a loop. She remembered the panic she'd felt when Max noticed the Black file, the expression of disappointment on his face when he realized the depth of Rosemary's deception, and the cold look in his eyes when he questioned their relationship and slammed the door in her face.

You just can't help yourself, can you? If you're always going to do whatever you please, no matter the consequences, maybe none of my feelings matter anyway.

Max wasn't wrong, but he wasn't exactly right, either. Or was he? Was their relationship automatically doomed because she couldn't let him take the lead?

Being in charge came as naturally to Max as breathing, and it was one of the things she admired most about him. He was a trained officer, a man of action, and she couldn't imagine him any other way. Unfortunately, it was also one of the qualities that caused the most friction between them.

Rosemary was, after all, a *woman* of action, and she wouldn't apologize for the trait any more than she expected Max to apologize for his personality.

She knew what Vera would say, but what did Vera really know about it? She and Frederick had no secrets because they'd been friends far longer than lovers, and besides, neither of them had any reason or desire to bother hiding anything from one another anyway.

And it wasn't as though she *fancied* being dishonest with Max. In fact, she thought indignantly, if he didn't want her to lie, perhaps he ought to be more understanding when she told the truth! Still, she knew that was selfish, or at the very least self-serving, and it wasn't in Rosemary's character to abide either one.

Could they figure out a way to coexist? One that didn't involve her deceiving him or him feeling the need to push her out of his professional life. What if she *did* decide to dust off the plaque Andrew had made for her before he died? The one that said, "Rosemary Lillywhite, Private Investigator?"

What if she decided to be the lady detective her late husband once believed her to be? Would Max be as accepting as Andrew had been? Rosemary didn't know the answer to that question, but she had a sinking feeling that if it was no, it would be the end of the relationship.

She wasn't going to pretend to be someone she wasn't. If Max wanted a pliable, compliant lady, he could throw a stone and hit an acceptable candidate, but Rosemary knew her only response to that would be to duck and take cover.

Shame battled with righteousness during the twenty or so minutes until she began to drift off, and the last thing

74

she heard before she fell into a fitful sleep wasn't her own internal battle but the caw of a crow perched just outside the bedroom window.

CHAPTER NINE

Unfortunately, all the sleeping draught did was ensure Rosemary slept on when the nightmares began. Garrison Black stalked her in her sleep, a shadowy figure always lurking over her shoulder, his breath hot on her neck. When he opened his mouth to speak, what came out was the desperate, shrill caw of a crow that sent shivers up and down her spine.

Rosemary woke in a pool of sweat and wasn't surprised to see only the faintest hint of daylight shining through her bedroom window. The house below was silent, and when she looked at the clock on her bedside table, she realized none of the staff—not even Gladys, who often arrived before dawn—had yet to stir.

She put on a pair of slippers and wrapped up in a thick dressing gown for warmth, then padded downstairs with the vague notion of fixing herself a cup of tea. Through the window facing the back garden, Rosemary could see that the lawn was still coated in a layer of dew, the sun's rays not yet having made their rounds to that section of the property.

For a few moments, she stood there enjoying the view and the peace and quiet that came with it. Her artist's brain surveyed the terrace; if she added comfortable seating and cleaned up the dingy set of dining furniture, it could become a place to enjoy breakfast or an afternoon with a good book.

If her suspicion that Wadsworth was responsible for placing the Garrison Black investigation information in plain sight of Max, she'd feel no remorse about turning the project over to him even though she knew he abhorred outdoor-related tasks.

The kettle began to whistle, and Rosemary moved to fetch it from the stove but stopped in mid-turn when something on the other side of the garden caught her eye. The gate leading to the park—the one the workers used to avoid traipsing through the house—had been left slightly ajar.

Perhaps, when they'd left the previous evening, the last one through had been careless with the latch. Rosemary contemplated marching across the garden but looked down at her slippers and decided she was inappropriately dressed for a stroll across the dewy lawn. When the workers arrived, she would remind them to double-check the gate before leaving at the end of the day.

Rosemary removed the kettle from the stove, poured boiling water into the pot, and leaned in for a whiff of fragrant steam. Dash came trotting into the kitchen just as she placed the lid. His fur was disheveled, much like Rosemary's hair, and she smiled at the sight of him.

"Good morning to you," Rosemary said, following the pup's longing gaze towards the door leading out to the terrace. She nodded in understanding and resigned herself to her fate before swapping her slippers for a pair of rain boots standing near the entrance.

She didn't dare let Dash loose in the garden with the gate ajar, particularly given his propensity for chasing the birds away from their perches, so she sighed and pulled a lead from one of the coat hooks and attached it to his collar.

"Let's go," Rosemary said and pushed open the door expecting to be met with a view of the feeder where the crows enjoyed her daily offerings.

Instead, she was greeted by a sight that would have caused a scream to rise up in her throat had she not already seen her fair share of bodies—because that's exactly what was sprawled across Rosemary's terrace.

Given the positioning of the limbs, she couldn't see the face, but she could tell it was a man from the style of clothing and the sheer bulk of the figure. One arm protruded from beneath a thin, shabby overcoat that smelled of vomit and made Rosemary's own stomach flip over. She reached down to check for a pulse but realized quickly it was too late for that. The man was dead as a doornail—splayed out across her terrace!

Dash let out a whine that roused Rosemary from her calm examination of the scene, and she came back to herself with a start. Had she given in to instinct and let out some sort of exclamation, help might have already arrived in the form of Wadsworth or perhaps one of her neighbors. Since she had refrained from doing so, Rosemary now found herself in a rather unsettling position.

She couldn't very well let Dash contaminate the scene, so she brought him inside and, with a sincere apology, corralled him in the pantry. "I'll be right back," she promised, hoping he wouldn't do his business on the floor but deciding if he did, it would be the least of her problems.

With shaking hands, Rosemary dialed the police station and explained the situation. She felt fortunate to have recognized the operator's voice and grateful when Jeanine promised to ensure Max was alerted immediately. That Jeanine didn't sound surprised to have received such a call from Rosemary was somewhat unsettling, even if it was entirely justified.

Rosemary could only imagine what everyone at Max's station thought of her, and for a brief moment, she felt a sliver of remorse for causing him strife. Then she remembered how many potential victims she had saved by what Max considered *meddling* and decided she would rather be labeled a thorn in the side of the London constabulary than respected as a proper lady.

She hurried back to the rear of the house, nearly skidding into Wadsworth, who'd entered the kitchen looking fresh as a daisy despite the still-early hour.

"Good morning, my lady. Is something the matter?" he asked sharply, forgetting his perfect manners for a fraction of a second, distracted as he was by his mistress's appearance. It wasn't often any of the staff, save for Anna as her personal maid, saw Rosemary looking anything less than smartly put-together.

"You aren't going to like it," Rosemary warned in answer. "Come look." She ushered Wadsworth to the back door and out onto the terrace where her butler's eyes darkened. "I've called the police, and I didn't touch him other than to check for a pulse. He's most definitely dead."

Wadsworth, a former policeman himself, walked around the figure in a wide arc. While he did so, Rosemary took another look at the scene, answering his rapid-fire questions distractedly.

"I've no idea who he is or how he came to be in my garden. Most likely, through the open gate, or perhaps he's responsible for that himself. As for the cause of death, I'll leave that determination up to the coroner. It's bad enough to have found him here, and if he didn't die of natural causes, well, I'd prefer to keep my hands clean for the time being."

She didn't add that she'd already, just the previous evening, landed herself firmly on the chief inspector's bad side. Somehow, she had a feeling Max wouldn't be pleased to have to return to her home so quickly after their fight, particularly for a reason such as this. A dead body on her doorstep, indeed!

At least it was the back door, Rosemary thought, and not the front where the entire neighborhood would have been privy to the sight. Then again, perhaps out front, someone else might have found him, alerted the police, and spared her from being the one to discover the poor dead man.

By the time Max arrived, Rosemary had cleaned herself up—she certainly didn't want to be seen in her dressing gown by the coroner or any of the constables, not to mention Max!—and Dash, unsettled by the commotion, had been appropriately walked and relegated to the study.

Max appeared not to have slept any more soundly than Rosemary had, and it looked as though he'd also dressed quickly. His suit wasn't as sharp as usual, and he'd missed a loop when fastening on his belt.

His eyes—uncertain and still quite stormy—met Rosemary's and, after a moment, softened infinitesimally. "Are you all right?" he asked quietly when she'd finally managed to force her feet to propel her to his side.

"Quite," Rosemary assured, attempting a thin smile that caused Max's mouth to press into an even thinner line.

Of course, Rosemary was fine—this type of situation was old hat to her, after all. The uncharitable thought crossed Max's mind and immediately left a stain of shame there. It wasn't her fault she'd had to learn to steel herself, and he knew his indictment was too harsh—much as it was the previous evening, but now was not an appropriate time to offer his apology. He had a job to do, and his private life would simply have to wait.

Rosemary watched Max's expression shift through his emotions, each one a knife to her heart. She hardened, but kept her face impassive and got down to business. "Come with me. Wadsworth has been standing guard over the scene."

Max nodded and then opened the front door and poked his head out. "Clayton, let's go," he said sharply.

The young constable skipped up the steps and followed Max inside, bowing his head to Rosemary sympathetically. "Sorry for your loss, Mrs. Lillywhite."

Max sighed. "She doesn't know the dead man, Clayton," he explained with annoyance. "She merely discovered the body."

"Oh," the constable said, blushing scarlet.

Rosemary shot an exasperated look at Max. Why he was acting so churlishly towards such a nice young man was beyond her comprehension. "Thank you for the sentiment, constable. I appreciate the overture. Not all men are so attentive to a woman's feelings," she said pointedly before turning on her heel and leading the way through the dining room to the kitchen and the door Wadsworth guarded.

Ignoring the dig, Max followed behind. His brow furrowed when he caught sight of the body, the crease between his eyes growing deeper as he walked around it and examined the scene.

"Is anything out of place?" he asked, indicating the garden with a wave of his hand.

Having already taken stock of every detail, Rosemary replied immediately and succinctly. "The gate was ajar when I arrived in the kitchen just after sunrise—I glanced at the clock in the hallway on my way, and it showed a quarter past five. The easterly end of the garden is visible through the kitchen windows, and I assumed the workers had left it unlatched when they left yesterday evening."

Before Max had a chance to ask, Wadsworth spoke up. "For once, my lady, you are incorrect. The gate was most definitely closed when the men cleared off. I took

Dash that way for his evening constitutional and fastened it up behind me."

"That settles that," Rosemary acknowledged, taking one last look about while Max noted down the details of Wadsworth's account. "It surprised me to see the gate ajar, given how vigilant the workers are regarding their evening cleanup. All their tools have been relegated to the area near the potting shed." She indicated a neat row of garden implements leaning against the shed's exterior wall behind the parked wheelbarrow and reassured him, "Nothing else has been disturbed."

Max nodded once and slipped his notebook back into his breast pocket just as the sound of the coroner's van could be heard pulling up at the front of the house. While Wadsworth went to fetch him, Max took off his coat and asked Rosemary to hang it on one of the hooks inside the door.

"Perhaps you ought to stay inside, Rose," he suggested, "while I turn him over."

This she brushed off with an irritated scowl, though when Max moved the beefy arm and rolled the body over, Rosemary suddenly and violently wished she'd taken his advice.

It was a visage she would have recognized anywhere, even with nearly half of it covered by a thick tangle of beard.

Her eyes flicked from Max's face to that of the dead

man and back, her mouth opening and closing soundlessly several times before her world flickered and went dark.

Max watched helplessly as Rosemary's eyes rolled back, and she fainted. He tried to lunge towards her but could only watch as she began to fall. And then, suddenly, she seemed to hang in the air for a moment before he realized she'd been caught from behind by Wadsworth, returning with the coroner in tow.

"My lady!" Wadsworth cried, his voice panicked.

"She's only fainted," Max explained. This Rosemary heard as she came back to herself with a start. Indeed, she'd only been out for a short moment—just long enough to be rendered utterly mortified.

She tried to get up, but Wadsworth couldn't be swayed. "What's happened?" he asked tersely, the question directed towards Max rather than his mistress.

"We've identified the body; that's what's happened," Max replied. "And you're not going to believe it, but it's Garrison Black."

CHAPTER TEN

Rosemary stood, just as soon as they'd let her, but it required a great many protests that she was, indeed, just fine. Her pride had taken a beating, but otherwise, she was perfectly unharmed.

It wasn't until Vera arrived in a flurry, Frederick at her heels, and insisted Rosemary be allowed to speak for herself, that the fanfare following her Victorian swooning episode dissipated. Oh, the horror!

"How do you suppose he died?" she asked the coroner, who had merely watched in amused silence while the chief inspector fawned over Rosemary.

The coroner consulted his clipboard. "I saw no signs of a struggle or any life-threatening injuries. Minor scrape to the head, consistent with a fall—most likely occurring during his collapse. He's no pillar of health, certainly. My best guess would be heart failure, but I'd need to perform an autopsy to be certain, and quite frankly, I'm disinclined to allocate the resources." He then turned to Max. "Officially, it'll be deemed death by natural causes. Lucky, that, for you lot, I suppose. Nice and tidy; one more mass murderer off the streets of London."

Max merely nodded, but to Rosemary's eye, he appeared relieved, and she supposed she ought to feel the same way. After all, the coroner was right. Garrison Black was dead, his threat against Rosemary no longer a concern. She could stop looking over her shoulder. She could stop investigating behind Max's back.

Drat it all! Rosemary thought to herself. Had Wadsworth waited a mere handful of hours more, Max need never have known she'd been investigating behind his back in the first place. The old adage that the 'right hand giveth and the left hand taketh away' crossed her mind, and she silently cursed the coincidental nature of life.

Rosemary filled in Vera and Frederick on the details of her morning while Max took notes and Wadsworth continued to stare at Garrison Black's face until it disappeared beneath the coroner's white sheet. Rosemary couldn't fathom what must be running through his mind. Garrison Black was the reason Wadsworth had left police work years ago, and in a roundabout way, was the reason he'd been arrested for murder just a few months prior.

She'd solved the case and saved Wadsworth from the

gallows, but Rosemary knew it had wounded his pride. Now, the whole ordeal was over, and even though she felt a great sense of relief, Rosemary couldn't seem to convince her stomach to settle.

"Clayton, go take a look at the gate. See if it was forced. We have to be thorough," Max said, nodding towards his constable.

The coroner raised a brow, "Clayton, you say? Any relation to Bernard Clayton of the—"

"No, sir," the constable stuttered, cutting the coroner off mid-sentence. "I've no family to speak of." He left it at that and sauntered towards the gate while the coroner and Max both shrugged and shook their heads.

The pair returned to the task at hand while Rosemary walked a little further on, just out of earshot on the other side of the garden where her brother and Vera stood. She watched as Max and the coroner engaged in a short discussion, noticing every time one of their concerned gazes shifted in her direction.

Soon, she thought, perhaps those concerned gazes would disappear entirely, and she could go back to living her normal life.

Perhaps she could stop finding dead bodies altogether.

As the coroner's van pulled away from the curb, Anna arrived for her workday. She rushed inside in a panic, eyes wide, a worried expression painted across her face. After taking stock of the party assembled at the table and ascertaining that nobody was missing, relief flooded her features.

"Was that the coroner I saw leaving just now? What's happened?" she asked before catching sight of Constable Clayton and flushing scarlet.

Rosemary wondered, idly and perhaps inappropriately, whether his and Anna's evening had gone any better than hers and Max's. The previous night felt as though it had happened much longer ago than a mere handful of hours, she decided warily.

Anna avoided the constable's attempt at eye contact and turned instead to her mistress. "Miss Rose, is everyone all right?"

"Indeed," Rosemary replied, crossing the room to place a comforting hand on Anna's shoulder. She pulled the girl onto a chair and explained what had transpired that morning while Dash, having finally been let out of seclusion, hopped into Anna's lap and began licking her chin excitedly. She admonished him lightly, set him down on the floor, and shooed him out of the dining room while still listening intently to Rosemary.

"So, you see, it's over," Rosemary concluded, "a blessing, really. Garrison Black can't hurt me or anyone else ever again. That means you're safe as well, thank heavens."

She had worried over the safety of her staff, and ever since the business with Black began, had tried to keep

Anna as far away from harm's way as possible. It was a relief to know she could cease with much of the worrying that had plagued her these last months.

"It's wonderful," Frederick echoed the sentiment through a bite of buttered toast. "We can all stop thinking about and, even more importantly, talking about Garrison Black. Case closed, isn't that right, Max? You must feel relieved."

Max did indeed appear relieved and also somewhat uncomfortable, given he and Rosemary still hadn't found a chance to speak privately since their fight the previous evening. A lot had changed in the meantime, and now he found himself breakfasting with her, Frederick and Vera, and to top it all off, the constable-in-training with whom he'd quite rather have maintained a strictly professional relationship.

Unfortunately, on that count, social niceties had trumped his desires—and that wasn't all they'd done. It was plain to see that Anna, who had arrived to work rather than breakfast with her employer, was unsure how to proceed with the handsome constable watching her every move.

As soon as he could, Max excused himself and veritably dragged the young Clayton off with him. "I'll call on you soon," Max said to Rosemary, formally, at the front door before ducking out.

Well, thought Rosemary, *perhaps that's that*. From the

dining room, she could hear Frederick's boisterous voice and suddenly felt incredibly exhausted. She glanced at the clock on the wall at the end of the hallway and realized it was only half-past-nine in the morning. Already she felt as though she'd spent a whole day doing something physically demanding, such as following Vera on a dizzying chase around the shops.

Nevertheless, a task even more tiring than that required Rosemary's immediate attention. She left Frederick and Vera to their breakfast, sat down at the telephone desk, and rang her parents' house in Pardington, hoping against hope that by some miracle, her father might answer her call.

It was not to be so, and only too late did Rosemary remember Mr. Woolridge was currently working in the London office, bringing Frederick up to speed on the family business. At least that meant her brother wouldn't be hanging around all day; he had places to be and the family patriarch to answer to.

Truth be told, Frederick had become much more responsible since settling down with Vera than Rosemary had ever dreamed he would. She was proud of him, of course, and grateful he'd stopped getting into trouble that she was invariably forced to set right.

"Rosemary?" Evelyn's voice came over the line in a shout, as always. "What's wrong, dear? It's not your brother, is it?"

"Why must something be wrong?" Rosemary retorted, shaking her head even though her mother's assumption was correct. She didn't bother to add an inquiry as to why Frederick's wellbeing was more important than anyone else's, as family history had already made her acquainted with the answer to that question.

Ever since their eldest brother was killed in the war, Frederick had become the last hope for the good Woolridge name, something their parents cared about deeply. Rosemary couldn't very well blame them on that count, but it did often make her and her sister, Stella, feel like they were both competing for second fiddle.

From all the way out in the countryside, Evelyn huffed, bringing Rosemary back to the conversation at hand. "You never ring this early in the day; in fact, you rarely ring at all unless there's a crisis of some sort. I assume today is no different." She sounded mildly hurt, a fact her daughter promptly ignored. Acknowledging Evelyn's exaggerated pain would only lead to a guilt trip—one she'd already taken more times than she cared to count.

"It's good news, of a sort," Rosemary explained. That's how her mother would see it, anyway. "Garrison Black is dead."

Silence held the line for a long moment. "That is a relief," Evelyn finally replied. "You must feel as though a great weight has been lifted from your shoulders."

It was a far calmer reaction than Rosemary had expected. The moment she'd learned of Black's death threat, Evelyn had attempted to lure Rosemary back to Pardington, where she felt her daughter would be safest. Now that it was a moot point, there went Evelyn acting as if the threat hadn't been a serious concern in the first place. Sometimes Rosemary wondered if her mother acted this way on purpose.

Rosemary almost ended the conversation without relaying all the details, but she thought better of it in the end and explained how—and where—the body was found.

"My heavens," came another of Evelyn's nonchalant reactions, much to Rosemary's irritation. She then changed the subject. "You ought to call your sister and explain it all to her yourself. She's been an absolute pill. Lately, I'll warn you now. Whenever I suggest something nice for the baby's nursery, your sister tells me I'm *out of touch with the latest fashions*. Yellow and green, indeed! What if it's a girl, I ask you?"

Rosemary wished she could turn back the clock and task Frederick with the chore of calling their mother. Since that wasn't an option and thanks to a lack of sleep and an excess of excitement, she let a comment slip from her lips that, under normal circumstances, she might have kept to herself.

"Is Stella's nursery decoration really of the utmost

importance this morning, Mother? I've just told you I found a dead body in my garden."

"What is it you need from me, dear?" Evelyn replied with a sigh. "If I waited until you weren't up to your ears in dead bodies, I'd never speak to you at all. At least this time, there's no investigation for you to involve yourself in. Perhaps now, you can get your life back on course."

She'd no idea what *getting her life back on course* meant, but knowing her mother, it was likely a euphemism for finding another husband. From Evelyn's viewpoint, Rosemary was practically an old maid!

"All this talk about going to America. Honestly, who even considers traveling across the sea with two babies in tow?"

People did it all the time, Rosemary thought but didn't say out loud—entire families, in fact, with far less posh accommodations than those the great college of Oxford would bestow. Stella, her professor husband, and of course their children would be ferried across the Atlantic in style and comfort, and truth be told, Rosemary envied her the opportunity.

Of course, she'd miss her sister and worry for her safety, but that didn't mean Stella ought not to go. She wished her mother felt the same way, and could simply wish her daughter safe travels, but Rosemary knew that was too much to hope for.

Evelyn waxed on for a while longer, no replies necessary, and then made yet another comment about Frederick's accomplishments—a comment that made her blood boil. Even though she was seething, Rosemary continued to keep her thoughts to herself and let her mother wind down.

"Tell Vera to ring me, please," Evelyn said just before disconnecting the line, "and also ask her to remind that new housekeeper of theirs she needs to ensure my messages are delivered. It's the only explanation for why Vera hasn't returned my calls, and it's unacceptable."

Rosemary doubted very much that Vera had missed Evelyn's messages and could think, off the top of her head, of several other explanations as to why she had yet to return Evelyn's calls. Thankfully, her mother had already hung up because Rosemary wasn't sure she possessed the strength to refrain from saying as much.

Exasperated, she reentered the dining room just as Frederick was preparing to leave for the office. Deliberately, she kept her mother's request to herself; Vera would return the telephone calls when she felt like it, and no sooner. Evelyn's insistence might actually increase her wait time if Vera was feeling particularly vindictive.

"Until tonight, my love," Frederick boomed, kissing Vera fully on the lips and then dropping a peck on his sister's cheek on his way out the door. "Get some sleep, Rosie," he said with an impish grin, "you look like hell."

Chapter Eleven

Vera's insistence on leaving Rosemary to get some rest did not, she assured, have anything to do with Frederick's impudent comment.

"It's been a long morning," she said gently. "Let Anna draw you a bath, then fall into bed knowing your world has been set back to rights again. We'll celebrate later, even if it does seem rather a macabre event to celebrate. Find out when Max is free, and we'll plan another evening out."

That Vera could, given recent events, be considering another night on the town came as no surprise to Rosemary. She'd no illusions regarding her friend's resilience, but there was one thing Vera still didn't know. Rosemary hadn't yet found an opportunity to fill her friend in on the current status of her relationship with Max.

She came quite close to spilling the details right then but ultimately decided it was a longer conversation that could be had when her eyes weren't drooping into her tea. With a murmured, noncommittal reply, she let Vera continue babbling on about the good fortune of Garrison Black having dropped dead on Rosemary's doorstep.

It seemed everyone around her felt the same way; everyone except Rosemary herself, who would have preferred a quiet morning and to hear about Black's death via the headlines, along with the rest of London. Truly, couldn't he have collapsed on the next street over?

"I'll come back this afternoon to check on you, Rosie," Vera said, interrupting Rosemary's thoughts as she repeated Frederick's gesture and kissed her friend's cheek before taking her leave.

Grateful for the reprieve, Rosemary headed towards the stairs to her bedroom. On impulse, as she passed the telephone stand, she picked up the folder with the notes on the Black case and threw it, forcefully, into the bin. Out fluttered the charcoal drawing of herself, and Rosemary thought again how much nicer it would be for Black to have died in someone else's garden.

A truth that had circled her mind all morning suddenly flashed brighter than a neon light and took her breath away. She had been spared; Garrison Black had been poised to enter her home but died before he had the chance to carry out his intention of killing her—an intention he'd made quite clear with his threatening notes and disturbing drawings.

How close, exactly, had she come to being murdered in her own bed? Would anyone have come to her rescue? Dash, despite his inclination to bark at the slightest noise, slept like a log. He probably wouldn't have stirred even in the event of an intrusion, and while his spirit was willing, his diminutive size made him an unlikely protector.

The notion sent a shiver up Rosemary's spine, and for a moment, she felt completely daft. Had that been what Max and the coroner were discussing during their examination of the scene? She must be deeper in shock than she realized; it was the only explanation for her being so slow to put the pieces together.

It didn't much matter, anyway, she decided, since Black was dead now. However close he'd been to making her his next victim, he hadn't succeeded. Somewhere deep down, Rosemary knew she was finally safe, and she let the realization wash over her like ocean waves. She was safe, yes, and also very, very tired.

She stood contemplating for a long few moments, then pulled the folder out of the bin and changed her trajectory from one staircase to the other. Instead of going up, she went down to the ground floor studio office and laid out the file and the drawings next to the journal Esme had found amongst her late husband's things.

Rosemary took a deep breath and then tucked the lot into a drawer, vowing to return once she'd regained her strength and dispose of it and the rest of the case files. Perhaps she would clear out everything related to detective work and start entirely fresh, just as she'd intended to do before Grace Barton had come searching for someone to take on the case at Barton Manor so many months ago.

If Rosemary had said no at the time, she'd never have been in this position, to begin with. Yes, walking away from detective work was the right decision; she could reconcile with Max and wipe her hands clean of both Garrison Black and murder investigations at the same time.

She slammed the desk drawer with finality and ascended the stairs feeling lighter than she'd felt in a long time. Sleep would take care of the rest; would blow out the cobwebs so she could finally find some peace.

Chapter Twelve

Blessedly, that night, nightmares chose not to stalk Rosemary. No looming figure lurked over her shoulder; the ghost of Garrison Black no longer haunted her dreams. She slept soundly and woke the next morning feeling rested for the first time in longer than she could recall.

She hummed while she dressed and readied herself for the day, stopped to give Dash a good scratch behind the ears when he met her at the bottom of the stairs and entered the dining room with a spring in her step. Her mother was right; Rosemary did feel as though an enormous weight had lifted from her shoulders.

The morning paper featured a sizable headline with a snippet-sized story. *An end to the madness! Mass murderer Garrison Black is dead!*

Rosemary read the article out loud:

Garrison Black, the mass murderer who terrorized the city for over a decade, eventually murdering six young women and police constable Benton Greene, has topped the wanted list ever since he escaped a London jailhouse six months ago. Today, his reign of terror has finally ended.

According to Chief Inspector Maximilian Whittington of the London constabulary, Black perished from natural causes, specifically heart failure. The inspector went on to say that "justice has been served," and the multiple murder case against Black is now closed.

Black's body was discovered early yesterday morning by Rosemary Lillywhite of Marylebone, London who, last November, helped clear the name of one Carrington Wadsworth, the ex-officer who stood accused of the murder of police sergeant Nathaniel Prescott.

Mrs. Lillywhite has also assisted in solving several other cases both in London and the country village of Pardington, where her family resides.

Just then, the telephone bell jingled, and it didn't stop for the rest of the day.

The first to call was Evelyn, far less uninterested than when Rosemary told her about discovering Black's body. Somehow, it hadn't occurred to her mother that given the circumstances, Rosemary's name would be in all the papers, and now Evelyn wanted to hear every detail—no doubt to relay to the ladies in her social circle, who were always on the lookout for a scintillating story.

Then came the calls from concerned friends—little more than veiled attempts to gossip (at least Evelyn was honest about it), save for a spare few such as Ivy Gibson and Esme Prescott. They, Rosemary was sure, truly cared how she fared.

Most of the calls were from members of the press. Journalists from every newspaper and magazine in England wanted an exclusive story from the woman who'd found Garrison Black's body on her doorstep.

Rosemary thought it best to speak to them directly, but Wadsworth stepped in to act as the voice of reason. "One never can be certain when it comes to the press. At least speak with the good inspector before you speak with any journalists."

Coming from Wadsworth, the term 'good inspector' quirked Rosemary's brow. Of course, Wadsworth respected Max's station; he was a former officer himself and a man who valued rules and order. However, as the relationship between Max and Rosemary deepened, Wadsworth had taken on a fatherly, protective role when it came to his mistress.

For once, Rosemary listened to his advice and waited impatiently for Max to arrive and provide some sort of guidance. The station operator had indicated she might be waiting a while, as Max was inundated with tasks related to the closing of the Black case.

Slightly irritated, Rosemary accepted an aptly-timed call from Max's mother, Ariadne. "Your ears must have been ringing by proxy," she commented into the speaker. "We were just discussing your son, though I don't expect to see him anytime soon given the circumstances."

"I rather think you're correct on that count," Ariadne agreed, but her tone was sympathetic enough to calm Rosemary's worry that Max had filled her in on their falling out. He tended to, like most sons, tell his mother no more than the most pertinent points of his life, and for that, Rosemary was grateful.

"I just rang to congratulate you, my dear. How terribly exciting, and what a coup! You've done what the London constabulary couldn't—caught a murderer! I'm quite proud of you, you know. I've told all the ladies at the garden club, and everyone in my new bridge club, of course, that my son is courting the lady who foiled Garrison Black!"

Steam nearly poured out of Rosemary's ears. "Ariadne! That's simply not true. I hardly foiled Garrison Black! He had a heart attack on my doorstep, that's all."

Ariadne brushed Rosemary off. "Someday, you'll be an old lady, and praise won't come as easy as it does to you now. Don't look a gift horse in the mouth."

Finding it better to just agree with Max's mother, Rosemary offered no rebuttal and instead begged off the call, promising to keep Ariadne apprised of any new developments that might be fodder for bridge night conversation.

Rosemary understood how busy Max must be, and though she hadn't expected to see him shortly, she was surprised when he failed to turn up at all that day. She placed a few more calls and left another message, but to no avail. Perhaps she'd fallen even lower on his list of priorities than she'd thought.

At Wadsworth's insistence, she avoided leaving the house all afternoon, keeping the drapes drawn and the doors tightly locked. In the garden, the workers followed Wadsworth's instructions to a T, ensuring all traces of the ordeal were removed and the lawn returned to its former glory.

Even the dingy dining room set she'd planned to use for tea on the terrace got a fresh coat of paint—an attempt at atonement, Rosemary was sure, for her butler's role in causing tension with Max.

Finally, after dinner, the telephone quieted, and she was able to enjoy a peaceful evening and a night of relatively undisturbed sleep. She woke to feel slightly less rested than the previous day, the niggling concern regarding Max's silence expanding in the morning light to linger like a cloud as she bathed and dressed.

Rosemary should have realized something was off when Anna avoided her gaze and tripped up the stairs with a mumbled excuse about pressing the bedroom curtains. Her intuition should have gone off like a siren when Wadsworth asked if she was certain she wanted to read the morning paper.

Neither of those things managed to penetrate her

consciousness, and it wasn't until Gladys poured her tea with an uncharacteristically sympathetic smile did Rosemary raise an eyebrow.

"Wait," she said as Wadsworth tried to slink out through the kitchen after the cook. "Out with it," she demanded, her tone brooking no refusal.

Wadsworth turned on a heel, handed his mistress a folded-up paper, and said simply, "Apologies, my lady." He then crossed his hands behind his back and lifted his nose in the air the way butlers tend to do, standing sentry whilst feigning disinterest.

Rosemary unfolded the paper in a huff, her eyes blazing in Wadsworth's direction while she muttered, "For goodness' sake, what am I? Made of glass? What I couldn't possibly handle—oh!"

Her eyes widened as she scanned the article, and suddenly Rosemary became incensed.

"This is positively ludicrous," she spat, throwing down the paper and pushing her still-full plate towards the center of the table in disgust. Unable to stop herself, Rosemary picked the paper back up a moment later.

Vera found her pacing a path in the dining room carpet, muttering to herself as she read. "Have you seen this rag?" Rosemary demanded as soon as Vera arrived. "*Garrison Black, dead as a doornail*, reads the headline."

Vera raised an eyebrow. "Garrison Black *is* dead,

Rosie," she replied.

"Indeed," Rosemary replied coolly, "but he didn't *meet his end at the hand of his latest would-be victim,* did he?"

According to a source, Garrison Black was stalking Mrs. Lillywhite, his focus having shifted from one heiress—Arabelle Grey—to another. It's no secret Black had a type, but that's now two victims who escaped his grasp.

Mrs. Lillywhite, however, is no regular victim. Over the eighteen months since her husband, a former police officer turned private detective, passed away, Mrs. Lillywhite has forced her way into several murder investigations.

Some in the department find Mrs. Lillywhite's assistance a nuisance. "She fancies herself a lady detective," one constable has stated, "but she's no Sherlock Holmes, to that any of our officers will attest."

"Of all the nerve!" Rosemary fumed. "Sherlock Holmes wasn't a *lady detective* either. Whoever this constable is, he's really got a way with words!"

While Rosemary paced, Vera followed behind her, mimicking her every move in a way that was downright uncanny and also quite irritating, especially given Rosemary's mood. The blood rose to her cheeks, and she bit back a sharp reprimand but pierced her friend with a look that brought Vera back to her senses.

"You're absolutely right to be angry, Rosie. They'll say anything they can to avoid revealing you didn't just *assist* in their investigations—you solved them singlehandedly! Whenever men are in power, which of course is *always*, they can't stop themselves from subjugating women in an attempt to maintain that power."

"Hey, now," Frederick interrupted, offended, "don't lump us all into the same category. I've no affiliation with this unnamed constable, and neither do I find a woman's intelligence off-putting. In fact, it gets my engine revving, if you know what I mean." He wiggled his eyebrows at his wife and received a pinch-lipped head shake in reply.

"We *always* know what you mean, Freddie," Rosemary waved her brother off and returned to the article.

> Did Mrs. Lillywhite, who had been threatened by Garrison Black shortly before his death, perhaps decide to go tit for tat? If so, some might be inclined to call her London's savior, but is there ever a justification for the work of a vigilante?
>
> The fact remains that in a murder investigation, true coincidence is a rarity. Garrison Black, having died of natural causes on his next victim's doorstep, is one too big to ignore. Furthermore, the would-be lady sleuth, Mrs. Lillywhite, seems quite likely to know exactly how to commit the perfect crime.

CHAPTER THIRTEEN

"Oh, good heavens," Vera breathed when Rosemary was finished reading.

"Good heavens, indeed!" Rosemary retorted. "If I were to plan a murder, I certainly wouldn't leave the victim in my own garden, now would I? That doesn't sound like something a criminal mastermind would do, does it? How can they get away with printing this rubbish?"

Frederick blithely answered the question. "It's the press, sister dear. They can print whatever they'd like, but that doesn't make it the truth. I hardly think Mother will feel the same. It will be a scandal for the ages, one which Father will duly ignore."

He sounded positively thrilled at the prospect, grinning widely as he greeted Rosemary with a quick pat on her shoulder. It was almost as if he were afraid to get too close. Frederick preferred to keep all of his appendages intact.

"They're painting me as a femme fatale!" Rosemary lamented as she threw the paper down on the table in disgust. "I'll be the black sheep of Marylebone!"

Vera shrugged off the comment. "Pish posh!" she said in a fair imitation of her mother-in-law. "Who cares what the stodgy old frumps around here think of you, anyway?"

"I care what Max thinks, and I care how it will make him look," Rosemary said, slumping back into her chair, any vigor she'd felt that morning draining away. "I care about bringing shame to my family. It won't be good for business, I don't expect."

Frederick chimed in at that. "You'd be surprised how well a scandal can increase sales, Rosie. Don't fret. This could be the best thing that ever happened to Woolridge & Sons. We could expand our operations." His eyes turned misty. "Finally break into the American market; make a fortune!"

Frederick finally noticed the silence that had fallen during his moment of verbal exuberance and came back to earth. "Or, it might have no effect whatsoever," he said with a shrug of his shoulders. "Regardless, it hardly matters now. It would be better to focus on finding out who leaked all this information to the press. How do you think they knew about the threats? Not many people are privy to that knowledge, are they?"

It was a question that had niggled at the back of

Rosemary's mind as well; she had simply declined to vocalize it. "No," she said now, "not many at all. Good thinking, Freddie."

"Must your tone always indicate an utter lack of confidence in my mental capacities?" Frederick replied dryly. "I'm not entirely incompetent, you know."

Rosemary absently but with affection patted him on the arm. "Of course you're not."

From then on, who might have gone to the papers was all she could think about. She unequivocally discounted anyone in her household, including Gladys, who'd only recently come into service after Rosemary was forced to fire her former cook. Perhaps Helen had sought retribution, Rosemary thought with relief before remembering she had let Helen go before Black's first threat arrived.

Certainly, neither of her parents would let word slip. Cecil Woolridge was adept at handling the press, and Evelyn wouldn't deign to comment, particularly not regarding her daughter's private life.

That left no other option—except one, and it was one Rosemary could live with even if it did have bigger implications than all the others.

By the time Max finally arrived later that afternoon, she'd worked herself into a state. He found her pacing back and forth across the parlor, the dregs of a cocktail in her hand even though the clock was still ages away from the appropriate hour.

Max himself looked harried, though in her state, Rosemary hardly noticed.

"Which one of them was it, Max?" she demanded the moment he stepped through the door. It occurred to him that he should have questioned Wadsworth's pitying expression, but it was too late by then. "Which one of your constables sold me for a shilling? Was it Clayton?"

Max stared at Rosemary as if she'd gone mad. "I assume you're talking about today's papers. You know they'll latch onto any angle. I'm sorry for what they said, but you can't possibly believe my men had anything to do with it, can you? Even Clayton, who, admittedly, makes me want to tear my hair out—you don't really think he's capable of something like that, do you?" Max took a step back and squared his jaw. Rosemary failed to see the warning sign.

"Whyever not?" she countered, clinging to her fear. "It isn't as though your agency has been a pillar of morality!"

Max didn't know if all of his men were trustworthy; someone *had* helped Garrison Black escape from jail, after all, not so long ago. However, he'd spent a lot of time and energy trying to ensure nothing like that happened again. Deeply did he resent the insinuation that he hadn't worked hard enough.

He sidestepped the comment in an attempt to diffuse

the argument rather than fan the flames and said firmly, "It will blow over, quite quickly, I imagine, so long as you don't put any stock in it."

Before she could stop herself, Rosemary retorted, "I've my family to consider, don't you understand that? My father's business to worry over. Why do you Whittingtons seem to think there's no such thing as bad press? Your mother was positively thrilled to find my name mentioned above the fold!"

"Let me see if I understand what you're saying, Rose." Max kept his cool even though it felt as though his head might explode. "You think either my men, the trusted few who were granted knowledge of Black's threat, or my aging mother who adores you, called the papers and leaked confidential information about a murder investigation?"

It wasn't often Rosemary got angry. Even less frequently did she take it out on someone who didn't deserve it, and never had she ever made a baseless accusation against someone who had shown her nothing but devotion.

She swallowed hard. Ariadne's involvement hadn't been what she'd meant to insinuate, but between the cocktail's haze and the stress of the situation, the words had popped out of her mouth, and she couldn't deny they sounded like the ramblings of an insane person.

"I never even told her about Black's threat on you,"

he thundered, his patience having flown. "She cares about you, and I didn't want her to worry. Now you accuse her of betraying you?"

"That's not what I meant!" Rosemary finally forced herself to exclaim. She tried to take it back, but Max's ears turned crimson, and she thought steam might begin pouring out of his nose. By now, she didn't know what she *had* meant to say and vehemently wished she hadn't said anything at all.

"Do you want to know what's wrong with you?" he asked coldly. "You have no self-control. You're always suspicious, and you can't take no for an answer. I'm sorry you've lost people, Rosemary. Truly. I know how difficult it's been for you and how much easier it is when you can take control—when death is a mystery you can solve. But enough is enough." Edging past annoyance, Max fisted hands at his side. "Bloody hell. Now I understand why Andy had to go into private work. Do you think he'd be proud of you now?"

She'd been prepared to apologize. Prepared to sacrifice herself on the altar of remorse and take it all back, but Max's words landed like a slap in the face—or worse, like a series of them.

You have no self-control, slap.

You can't take no for an answer, slap.

Your dead husband would be ashamed of you, slap slap.

The last one hadn't been Max's exact words, but close enough. He knew it, and he felt the same level of regret as Rosemary did for hers.

"I won't abide murder, Max, not for *anyone's* pride," she fired back. "You're acting as though I seek them out! I'd prefer to be left out of it all, but neither will I turn a blind eye."

Max sighed and ran his hands through his hair in frustration. "There isn't anything to turn a blind eye to! Let the press take their potshots. This isn't a murder investigation!"

"It's a good thing, that," Rosemary retorted. "Don't you think the possibility should have at least been questioned? Or is it just a coincidence his body ended up on my doorstep?" That she echoed the same words she so abhorred seeing in black-and-white print served as an ironic reminder of how out of control the argument had gone.

Again, Max had to rein himself in. "And who, precisely, do you think would be the prime suspect in that scenario? Someone who lives in your house— someone like you, perhaps, or Wadsworth? You've seen what can happen when theories are allowed to run wild. Leave it be, and the papers will find a new bone to play with. A murderer is dead. It's over and done with, and as far as I'm concerned, he deserved his fate. Good riddance!"

Adrenaline coursed through Rosemary's veins. Filled her with righteous indignation she knew, somewhere deep down, would soon dissipate, she spat, "Oh, so it's an eye for an eye then? You sound like a barbarian!"

She recognized the comment for what it was—absolutely ridiculous—but refused to back down, so Max chose to take the high road.

"Perhaps I'll speak to you when you've calmed down, Rosemary," he said pointedly and then strode from the room. Seconds later, she heard the front door latch click quietly closed behind him. Somehow, it sounded far more final than it had the night he'd stormed off and slammed it shut.

Chapter Fourteen

Rosemary spent some time after her second official fight with Max doing little besides wallowing and feeling quite sorry for herself, but a couple of days later, she woke to the sound of the crows squawking from the back garden. The image of Garrison Black's body sprawled across the doorstep returned in a rush, as she vaguely recalled hearing the same noises the night he ended up there.

If she let it, that image could ruin the outdoor oasis she had looked so forward to enjoying. Suddenly, she regretted avoiding the space and neglecting the birds and decided to make early morning amends.

It felt like deja vu when Rosemary padded downstairs—fully dressed this time—a few minutes later and made her way to the back door. Her eyes flicked in the direction of the window across from the stove to the gate that was indeed now securely latched, and she let out the breath she'd been holding in.

"Good morning, Miss," Gladys greeted Rosemary with surprise, not for her presence in the kitchen, as that had become a common occurrence, but for the early hour. "Would you like me to fix you some tea?" Gladys asked. She'd already begun to prepare for breakfast, the sideboard strewn with flour and eggshells.

In reply, Rosemary smiled. "I'll take a cuppa on the terrace shortly, once I've finished with the birds."

A brief discussion ensued regarding Rosemary's plans for the kitchen, with Gladys positively giddy about the prospect of updating the space. "An electric refrigerator, indeed!" she'd said, tottering happily off towards the dining room with a stack of clean linens.

Rosemary breathed another sigh of relief when she finally opened the back door to find the terrace clear and everything as it should be: gardening tools neatly put away; wheelbarrow leaning against the back of the potting shed; everything from the shrubs to the lawn smartly groomed. It looked like a park—better, even—and the sounds of chirping birds and tittering chipmunks only contributed to the effect.

Making no objection to her advance, the crows cocked their heads, peered up at her and the food bucket with interest. Rosemary shook out the bucket, depositing the cache of kitchen scraps on the ground at their feet. One of the birds sprang forward and nipped a piece of carrot peel with no hesitation, while the other began a dance of sorts. It hopped sideways in the direction of an enticing chunk of hardboiled egg, then away, as if testing the offering before finally claiming it with what Rosemary construed as a proud strut.

Her heart sank when she heard the sound of the gate latch and the crows' demeanor suddenly changed. As Jack ambled into view across the lawn, they took off into the air, their tittering turning to the loud, urgent caws the workman's presence always elicited.

"Sorry, Miss Rose," he said, noting her disappointed expression with remorse. "They fly off every time I get too close. Don't like me as much as they like you." He blushed and scurried off after Rosemary reassured him he'd done no harm.

She changed her course, puttering about the garden, and while she meandered, Rosemary's thoughts wandered to the stack of post and messages piled near the telephone. Every day, along with another damning article, had come a flurry of comments and requests.

Some were from women looking for assistance from another female, though there was one request from a man. He'd lost his wife's prized poodle and indicated the task of finding it ought to be one even a lady detective could successfully complete. That note Rosemary had thrown directly into the fireplace.

Others she'd held onto and pored over while contemplating the decision she'd made to divest herself of the 'lady sleuth' title once and for all. The decision had been a violent, visceral reaction to the trauma of finding Black's body, and Rosemary reserved the right to change her mind.

Now, with said title foisted upon her by the press, she resented being forced into the spotlight at a time when she ought to have been granted a modicum of peace. And yet, who else would help some of these women? Then again, she couldn't solve the problems of every lady in London, could she?

Rosemary's thoughts seesawed back and forth like that for quite some time, the weight of them following her onto the terrace and accompanying her for tea. She deliberately let the morning paper sit, front page facing down, next to the tray, and ignored it entirely.

Instead, she plopped an extra lump of sugar into her cup and let the sweetness wash over her tongue. She'd come to realize that initially, she had overreacted; eventually, the excitement over Black's death would die down. He *was* a mass murderer, and even if a contingency of London believed she'd dispatched him herself, Rosemary trusted Max's assurance that the investigation was definitively closed.

Vera, having finally been made privy to the whole sordid tale of woe regarding the now *two* heated arguments with Max, had taken Rosemary's side with positively no regrets. As endearing a quality as was her undying devotion, this time it served only as a reminder that Rosemary was nothing more than human, and she could, indeed, be wrong.

She owed Max an apology but wasn't yet ready to throw herself on the sword, knowing someone had betrayed her trust and that the most likely culprit was one of his own colleagues. Furthermore, she fretted over the notion that he might not accept said apology—that he might tell her, in no uncertain terms, to bugger off.

Rosemary lingered in the garden until Dash's bark echoed out into the air.

He'd barely stopped when the sound of an unfamiliar voice preceded its owner to the terrace. The expression on Wadsworth's face as he announced the new arrival indicated—only to his mistress, of course—his sincerest apologies.

"A Miss Briony Keller wishes to speak with you," he said by way of introduction, then took his leave with his eyebrow still quirked.

Briony Keller tucked a wisp of hair back into a severe bun set on the crown of her head. The dated style and faded color had Rosemary guessing the woman was in her forties. Briony moved slowly, an apologetic smile on her lips, as she made her way across the flagstones with the help of a cane, and Rosemary revised her estimate upward by a few years. Wondering at the reason for the visit, Rosemary noted Briony's clothing and accessories were of modest quality but meticulously cleaned and cared for.

Looking about appreciatively, Briony took a seat even though her host hadn't offered one and tucked the cane away beneath the table. "It's lovely to meet you, Mrs. Lillywhite," she said, peering enviously at the steaming cup of tea in front of Rosemary.

Anticipating the need, Gladys and her teapot arrived before anything other than the mildest pleasantries were exchanged. She served the guest as though she'd been expressly invited rather than having, as Rosemary correctly assumed, forced her way inside.

"How can I help you, Miss Keller?" she asked, maintaining a polite facade even though she suspected the knew the answer to the question. Everyone seemed to want something from her these days, and she doubted this new arrival would prove an exception.

"Please, call me Briony," she insisted. "If we're to be friends, we ought to use our given names, wouldn't you agree?"

Rosemary was grateful for being raised to display patience and politeness even when presented with challenging social situations. She may not have appreciated her mother's perspective during said lessons, nor her teaching methods, but the resulting ability to maintain a neutral expression regardless of provocation was precisely Evelyn's aim.

"Of course," she breezed, "call me Rosemary. Now, what brings you here today?" She didn't recall agreeing to become this person's friend, this person who had just rather baldly interrupted her morning.

Briony did not appear compelled to answer the question. Instead, she gazed thoughtfully around the garden and said, "What an enchanting spot you've created; I'd quite like to compliment your landscapers. They've done a lovely job."

"Yes, it's been rather a large project," Rosemary replied, following Briony's gaze to where the wheelbarrow sat, filled to the brim with potting soil, "but it's nearly finished. You were saying you came here for my help?" She tried to direct the conversation back to where it had started, and this time Briony reached into the handbag she'd set on the seat beside her and pulled out an envelope.

Her hand shook as she passed it over, and Rosemary softened slightly. The envelope had been torn open rather carelessly, with one corner completely missing. Inside was a folded notecard with a message written in letters cut out of the newspaper.

The clock is ticking. You're running out of time, it said.

"This arrived in my postbox last week. The police were rather unconcerned," Briony sniffed.

Rosemary could see why. Not the type of message

anyone would relish receiving; the threat was too vague to spur immediate action. Furthermore, she guessed the police had seen enough cut-out newspaper letters to last lifetimes.

"It's not much to go on," Rosemary hedged. "I'm not sure if there's anything I can do to help you."

Briony's face fell, but she nodded once and then rearranged her expression. "I understand. My apologies," she said, formal now. "I thought perhaps you'd be more sympathetic, given that you've also been through the unpleasant experience of being threatened, but I won't bother you again. You've enough to concern yourself with, finding a dead body on your doorstep. My heavens, what a shock that must have been! And then to find out it's the mass murderer Garrison Black, well, I would imagine it's taken quite a toll."

She shouldn't have been surprised, but Rosemary was momentarily taken aback. She'd been on the verge of softening—after all, Briony Keller had one thing right; she knew what it felt like to be watched from afar, threatened with harm. She knew what it meant to live in fear, and she wouldn't wish the experience on anyone.

Still, something about Briony's plea vexed. Had she just come to pump Rosemary for information about the Black case? Could she possibly have even been sent from one of the newspapers? The notion wasn't particularly shocking and probably the precise reason

Wadsworth had only reluctantly allowed the woman entrance. Now Rosemary would have to admit his concern over safety was justified.

"I'm coping just fine," was what she said out loud, smoothly and pointedly.

Briony gathered her things and stood up slowly, with great effort, just as Wadsworth emerged from the house and offered to show her out. In his hands, he held an envelope, the sight of which made Rosemary cringe. She'd had her fill of correspondence, and judging by the expression on Wadsworth's face, wasn't going to like this letter any more than the last.

She also wasn't the only one who noticed Wadsworth's demeanor; Briony peered curiously at the envelope as he handed it to Rosemary and then reluctantly followed him back into the house.

Rosemary opened the envelope and read the note inside, her jaw dropping further with every sentence until her mouth formed an O.

Chapter Fifteen

Dear Mrs. Lillywhite,

What gives you the right to take the law into your own hands? Are you any better than the public's perception of Garrison Black? He deserved a fair trial, a chance to tell his story and clear his name. You took that from him, and I dearly hope someone robs you of it in return. You ought to be ashamed of yourself.

The handwriting was small, cramped, but very neat, and Rosemary instinctively knew it had been penned by a woman. She ran a finger over the distinctive fleur-de-lis patterned header, then flipped the card over and noted the lack of a postmark with concern. When Wadsworth returned, he confirmed her suspicion.

"It didn't come through the post," he agreed. "I would advise caution at this juncture, and I would implore you to notify the inspector."

Rosemary reread the note and shook her head emphatically. "No," she declared. "This is not the same as the one from Black. It isn't even a threat, and I intend to treat it no differently than the other letters I've received this week."

"Madam, do you not find the timing rather coincidental? That Miss Keller, she was strange, was she not?"

There wasn't much point denying *that*, but Rosemary rejected the notion. "I'll admit, leaving a threatening letter on my doorstep while consulting me in regards to a threatening letter of her own would be either the most ridiculous thing I've ever heard—or the most ingenious. Regardless, if that lady is the person who penned this note, I don't think I've much to worry over. She couldn't hurt a fly."

"But, Madam—"

"Wadsworth," Rosemary interrupted, a warning in her tone, "the inspector is to be left out of this, are we understood?"

Wadsworth let out a long breath and then stepped back, averted his mistress's gaze, and nodded once. "Understood." He left her there, on the terrace, and though she tried to avoid acting like a tyrant with her butler, in particular, Rosemary couldn't abide him disobeying her wishes.

On his way back inside, Wadsworth opened the door to release Dash, who trotted up to Rosemary with his tail wagging. In his mouth, he held a piece of plaited rope tied into a knot on either end, which she took and flung across the lawn.

Dash raced after it, again and again until his chest heaved with the effort, and Rosemary was forced to bring the game to a halt. She took him back inside, filled his bowl with fresh water, and washed the dirt and slobber off her hands.

A short while later, Vera arrived to find her friend perched on a bench tucked into a secluded corner of the garden. "What a lovely spot, Rosie," she exclaimed, echoing Briony's earlier sentiment before plunking herself down with a contented sigh. "You can almost forget you're in the center of the city."

"That was the aim, certainly. I'm thrilled it's been achieved," came Rosemary's distracted reply. She opened her mouth to tell Vera about the newest note, this one left on her doorstep, but she didn't get the chance.

"I got it, Rosie!" Vera said. Rosemary looked at her more closely and realized her friend practically vibrated with excitement. "I got the part. I'm playing the lead!"

All thoughts of Briony Keller and Garrison Black flew from Rosemary's mind. She couldn't be more proud of Vera and truly hoped this play would be the big break her friend hoped for. Then she remembered the character was based, at least in Vera's mind, on Rosemary.

"The only black mark on the whole thing is that I'm to appear opposite Cora Flowers. She's been cast as the murderer, a rather pivotal role in the play. Our characters play a cat-and-mouse game until she attacks me during the showdown in the final scene. I've no doubt she'll be fantastic."

"I'm quite certain your performance will be even more spectacular," Rosemary assured her friend sincerely.

For once, Vera didn't brighten at the praise. Instead, she watched Rosemary's every move, miming her friend's gestures and expressions. In preparation for her audition, Vera had made a nuisance of herself with this sort of behavior. Now that she'd won the part, things would probably go from bad to worse. To test the theory, Rosemary reached up to tuck a lock hair behind one ear, then patted her own cheek.

Out of the corner of her eye, she watched Vera repeat the action and decided to have a little fun.

"Only time will tell," Vera replied as she repeated the complicated sequence of taps Rosemary made with her fingertips on the table.

"We'll need to execute the scene flawlessly to make the biggest impact on the audience, but I don't think she'll go easy on me. In fact, I think she hates me. I can't understand why since I've never been anything but pleasant towards her."

Having known Vera almost forever, Rosemary took the statement with a grain of salt. As sweet as can be when feeling complacent, Vera occasionally succumbed to moments of doubt. When feeling self-conscious or in a position to lose something she cared about as much as she did the *role of a lifetime*, Vera could come across as less-than-pleasant, and that was putting it mildly. It wasn't Vera's best trait, but it also wasn't one she frequently indulged.

Still having a bit of fun at her friend's expense, Rosemary affected a nervous twitch that traveled from her neck to her shoulders, and down to the tapping of one foot.

"She's odd, always scribbling away in that notebook of hers," Vera continued, her mime routine taking a bit more of her attention now that Rosemary had increased her efforts.

"My advice is this: pay no attention to Cora Flowers," Rosemary said, knowing full well Vera would do whatever it was she wanted no matter what good advice she received. "Just give the best performance you can give, and I'm sure you'll steal the show."

Vera nodded, bolstered slightly by Rosemary's words, then she frowned. "Are you quite all right, Rosie? I fear your nerves are wearing on you, and you've developed a bit of a twitch."

Vera failed to see the humor that sent her friend into peals of laughter at her expense.

"I'm sorry, darling. I couldn't help poking a bit of

fun."

Eyes narrowed, Vera decided to let it go, and then grinned. "I'll play you better than you do yourself."

"That's what I'm afraid of."

Before the curtain rose on opening night, Rosemary thought, she'd probably end up owing Frederick money, besides.

***

Later that evening, Rosemary received a telephone call—the first one of the day she deigned worthy to answer, given that it was from her sister, Stella.

"How are you doing, Rosie?" Stella asked, her voice full of sympathy. "No, Nelly, go on now," she said before Rosemary could answer. "It's time for your bath. Go see Nanny. You can talk with Auntie Rose later."

At that, an ear-piercing shriek caused Rosemary to pull the speaker away from her head. "Stella, it's all right. I'd love to say hello to my nephew."

She was surprised her sister could hear that statement, but the screaming ceased a moment later even though Nelly did not come on the line.

"He's got to learn to hear the word *no*, Rosie," Stella said sternly. Rosemary sensed her tone had more to do with parenting challenges than it did irritation at the suggestion, so she took no offense.

"You sound exhausted," Rosemary commented. "How are *you* holding up? Aren't you ready to burst?"

Stella groaned and replied, "She could come at any moment."

"She?" Rosemary asked, surprised. "Do you have a crystal ball I don't know about? Because if so, I'd like to ask it a few questions of my own."

With a grunt Rosemary interpreted as an attempt at laughter, Stella answered, "It's just a feeling I've got, or perhaps it's blind hope. I can't take another boy! Don't get me wrong, I love my son to pieces, but he's far more than a handful, and I'm exhausted."

Rosemary let her sister wind down and then inquired as to the reason for her call. "I'd lose my head if it wasn't attached," Stella excused herself when she was forced to admit she couldn't recall what she'd intended to ask her sister. "I suppose I only wanted to check in on you. Mother says you haven't returned her last two messages."

Even if her eye roll was silent, Rosemary's deep sigh could be heard across the line. "She's been an absolute pill. I'm sure she's told you all about how much of a disappointment and embarrassment I am," Rosemary sulked. For all her complaining, she did crave, as most children do, her mother's approval.

"Actually," Stella said archly, "she's quite proud of you, you know."

Wondering what she'd said to put that tone in her sister's voice (their common ground had always been the fraught nature of their relationships with Evelyn), Rosemary sputtered incredulously. "You couldn't prove it by me."

Having realized she'd sounded rather harsh, Stella softened. "I know, Rosie, but it's true. She's the only one who is allowed to criticize any of us; if the press were a single person, they'd have received a thorough tongue-lashing from Mother. As it stands, I suspect she's left curt messages with all the papers. She's behind you, Rosie, as are the rest of the family. Just this once, perhaps cut her some slack."

Stella begged off the phone soon after, but her words stuck with Rosemary for the rest of the night. She'd been so frustrated with her mother, perhaps she hadn't really given her the benefit of the doubt. Evelyn *had* been strict and often harsh; she also loved all of her children deeply, and Rosemary knew that to be true.

Perhaps Max's assessment was correct. Maybe Rosemary really was self-centered. The notion was a concerning one that she vowed to resolve, and her planned charitable outing with the LLV seemed like the best way to begin.

Chapter Sixteen

In an unexpected turn of events, Max rang Rosemary that afternoon to set up a date for the following evening. Given the state of things between them, he was hesitant, but Frederick had bowled him over with his insistence that they celebrate Vera's new role. He doubted Rosemary had filled her brother in on their recent disagreements, yet somehow Max felt Frederick knew something was wrong. Leave it to Frederick to try and fix things. The man was just as meddlesome as his sister.

Rosemary, in turn, sensed her relationship with Max rested on the knife-edge of a precipice. One wrong move could send them toppling in either direction, and since she wasn't entirely certain where they might land thought it best to remain upright for the time being. That being said, she was thrilled he'd softened and didn't spend an inordinate amount of time wondering what had prompted the change of heart.

Spending her day at the LLV's East End outing would

leave barely enough time to do a proper job of fitting herself out for a date. Thankfully, the moment Max asked, Rosemary decided on a floral-patterned spring dress she knew brought out the color of her eyes. Vera's latest forceful push into the shops saved the day.

With Vera off at play rehearsal, Rosemary would attend the LLV outing on her own. She urged the staff to take the rest of the day off and tripped out the door with a spring in her step. Whatever happened between herself and Max, her life would go on; losing Andrew had taught her that. The world would keep turning, and she would need friends and something to occupy her time— preferably, something worthwhile that didn't involve a murder investigation!

As per Esme Prescott's instructions, Rosemary had paired a modest, knee-length skirt with comfortable shoes that wouldn't blister her heels. Altruistic as their intentions were, few—if any—of the LLV ladies knew what to expect from London's seedier side. Rosemary had an idea appropriate footwear would be the least of their concerns.

On her way to her car, Rosemary ran into Abigail from next door, raised her hand in a wave, and changed her trajectory to offer a greeting. "How are you?" she asked with a friendly smile.

Abigail waved back and closed the space between them, but with a trace of hesitation that took Rosemary aback. "Doing well, and you?" she answered somewhat stiffly.

Rosemary cocked her head to one side and studied her neighbor's face. Abigail appeared uncomfortable, though she could hardly understand why. "I've been both better and worse," Rosemary replied out loud, shifting the bulky handbag into a more comfortable position. Esme's suggestion to bring a packed lunch for fear they wouldn't find an appropriate eatery hadn't helped lighten the load. "I'm running late, but would you fancy a cup of tea tomorrow afternoon?"

Abigail appeared momentarily relieved, and then her eyebrows drew together. "Perhaps. I'll have to check my diary," she answered. "Talk with you later," she added and then retreated back to her house.

"How odd," Rosemary said out loud, then shook the thought of Abigail's strange behavior from her mind while she settled into the driver's seat of the car. As she drove across town, Rosemary wondered if perhaps she ought to have brought some sort of weapon along and then decided she *had* been involved in one too many murder investigations.

You're silly, Rosemary told herself. *People visit the East End all the time and walk away unscathed. It's probably not at all what you're envisioning. It's the opposite side of London, for heaven's sake, not the Serengeti.*

Except, once she arrived, Rosemary realized she might as well be on the other side of the looking glass, for the East End was a world away from Marylebone.

There, at least in certain sections, people slept in the streets—or rather, in the alleys—on top of crates or behind makeshift structures that would do nothing, come winter, to keep the occupants warm. Rosemary's heart hurt thinking about how many of these men might have fought for England to ensure her way of life was preserved, and now here they were languishing in the streets. That it didn't seem fair was a sentiment agreed upon by the entire group.

"All right," Ivy explained when the fifteen—Mrs. Higgins had declined to attend—ladies had assembled in a car park that, according to the map she now yielded, wasn't far from the Shadwell Homeless Shelter. "It's just across from the Anglican church." Ivy pointed towards the skyline in a southerly direction. "See the spire?"

Rosemary glanced that way and wondered why Ivy had suggested they park so far away from the shelter. Before she could open her mouth to give voice to the question, the group set off, tittering nervously.

"Are we sure we know where we're going?" Dressed all in black, Hadley Walsh grumbled from somewhere near the back of the group when the church spire looked no closer after several minutes of walking. "We look ridiculous traipsing around down here."

Ivy didn't bother to turn around but held up one hand as if to wave off Hadley's concern. Rosemary, however, was struck by surprise. Hadn't Hadley been the one who picked up on Minerva's idea and pushed for this expedition in the first place?

"Hush up, Hadley," someone from the front of the queue said loudly. Rosemary couldn't tell who said what everyone else had been thinking, but she did notice Hadley's friend, Maddy, flush with embarrassment. Maddy picked up her pace, putting some distance between herself and Hadley, who merely shrugged and continued to scowl.

When she noticed Rosemary looking in her direction, Hadley didn't smile or even wave as she normally would. Instead, she pointed her nose in the air and avoided Rosemary's gaze. It was just as well, and Rosemary was honestly relieved not to have to entertain the girl for the entire day.

In solidarity, Rosemary quietly followed Ivy's lead, wending through the streets for another fifteen minutes until the group still wasn't close enough to see anything lower than the lantern section of the church steeple. A single crow stood perched on one of the scalloped ledges and reminded Rosemary of those from her back garden. She wondered wryly how many of London's church steeples provided shelter for opportunistic corvids.

"We're walking in circles," Hadley pointed out loudly, "and wasting our time. I doubt any of these men will even accept our help. We should just turn around and go home."

Esme Prescott tossed her a quelling look and said, "Nonsense. The way I see it, we've a better shot than anyone else. What man, even a down-on-his-luck ex-war serviceman, doesn't want to spend some time talking with a pretty lady? Especially a pretty lady offering a free lunch? I say we make the rounds and ply them with homemade baked goods," she suggested, indicating the bags they each carried. "They need this food more than we lot do."

That was how it came to be that fifteen perfectly coiffed ladies from the West End of London ended up marching down alleyways, handing out paper-wrapped sandwiches to anyone who looked in need of a meal.

Rosemary suspected many of them weren't even the war patriots her friends believed them to be, but it didn't matter. Finally, after what felt like hours, the group found themselves standing in front of a run-down building with a sign reading *Shadwell Homeless Shelter*.

"Look at that," Ivy gloated with a wink in Hadley's direction. "We found it after all. Let's go make ourselves useful."

It seemed a simple enough task, and so the group filed in through a dingy set of doors that looked as though they hadn't been scrubbed clean in at least a decade. According to the plaque above the entrance, the building had originally been an orphanage. Once meant to house and feed unwanted children, now it did the same for loads of ex-servicemen who'd sacrificed so much and were now considered unfit for polite society.

The unfairness of it steeled Rosemary against the pain in her feet (no footwear choice could have saved her aching arches) and against the pain in her heart. Pity would do these men no good, nor would its display ingratiate herself to them.

Inside, an elevated counter separated the entrance hall from the dining and kitchen areas. Through a set of windowed doors, Rosemary could see a long worktop piled high with dirty dishes.

A harried-looking woman stood up from her seat behind the counter. She hesitated, her eyes growing wide as she took in the group standing before her. "How can I help you, ladies?"

"We're actually here to help you," Ivy replied, walking forward to offer a hand. "I'm Ivy Gibson."

The other woman looked at Ivy's outstretched hand with curiosity but shook it anyway and then stepped back and crossed her arms. "Is that supposed to mean something to me?"

If Ivy was taken aback by the abruptness of the question, she didn't let it show and instead widened her smile. "I called several days ago, inquiring as to whether my volunteer group could be of service. The Ladies for London Vitality?"

Ivy explained how they'd come to be there, and when she finished, the woman let the silence stretch out long. "I'm Penelope," she finally said, "but everyone around here calls me Penny. If you really want to help, there's plenty to be done: washing, mending, serving. Take your pick."

It was a challenge, of that Rosemary was certain. Could she really blame Penny for her disbelief? It didn't appear as though the shelter was well-funded, and how often did a group of upper-crust ladies come knocking, offering their assistance? Most likely, Rosemary, though, *never*!

A couple of hours later, as she bent over a steaming sink full of the dirty dishes she'd noticed earlier, Rosemary realized that much like gardening, she found herself taking a certain amount of pleasure in the hard work. She'd been pampered her whole life, given luxuries the men here could only dream about, and though Rosemary didn't think she ought to feel guilty about that, she also knew how privileged she was and found comfort in the idea of giving something back.

Through the windowed kitchen door, Rosemary had a clear view of the entrance and dining halls. Seated at one of the long trestle tables on the other end of the hall, the profile of a man caught her attention and made her head spin. Her eyes stung with tears, and she had to blink several times in quick succession to avoid embarrassing herself.

Suddenly, she was incredibly grateful that Vera hadn't accompanied the group downtown. Had *she* come face-to-face with the man Rosemary couldn't tear her eyes away from, it would have been a great shock. He looked so similar to her brother Lionel that it shook Rosemary to her core.

Upon further inspection, the resemblance wasn't quite as marked as it was at first glance, she realized with relief when the man turned his head to one side and allowed her a full view of his profile.

Where Lionel's jaw had been chiseled as if from stone, this chin was swallowed up by a thick speckling of facial hair well on its way to becoming a beard. These eyes weren't the piercing blue of Lionel's either, but they held the same sort of haunted expression she'd noticed in her brother's the last time she'd seen him alive.

Rosemary couldn't fathom the idea of approaching the man. She merely watched until he'd finished his meal, carefully mopping every drop of broth out of the bottom of his bowl with the last bits of bread crust. When he'd finished and moved out of her sightline, Rosemary's eyes—if not her thoughts—returned to the entrance hall and the counter where Penny stood sentry. She remained there now, looking through a stack of papers with a worried expression on her face.

While Rosemary scrubbed, she watched as Penny looked up and greeted someone arriving through the entrance door, then did a double-take when she recognized the figure approaching the counter.

It was Morris Clayton, Max's young constable, though it took a moment for Rosemary to be certain, given he was wearing casual clothes rather than his police uniform. The pot she'd been cleaning dropped into the sink, thudding loudly as it made contact with the cast iron, the sound echoing loudly across the curved ceiling of the dining hall.

Constable Clayton looked up, and his eyes widened as he peered through the windows and recognized Rosemary. He seemed as taken aback at seeing her as she was at seeing him. He spoke a few words to Penny, his eyes flicking between her and Rosemary as Rosemary dried her hands and prepared to exit the kitchen.

Before she made it out to the entrance hall, he'd gone, the door swinging shut behind him. Rosemary stared after him, thinking it rather odd behavior, and then turned to Penny.

"What did that man want?" she asked on impulse, earning herself a brief, narrow-eyed glance.

Penny shrugged and averted her eyes. "Just an inquiry," she said evasively.

Rosemary's instincts told her it was more than that, but before she could press, Penny stalked away to speak to one of the other LLV ladies who waved for her attention from across the hall.

Returning to the dishes, Rosemary considered what she'd just seen. What was Max's constable doing down here in Shadwell? Obviously, he hadn't followed her to the shelter on Max's orders; he'd been in plain clothes and clearly not expected to see her there. What connection might Clayton have to a homeless shelter? Perhaps he hailed from the East End and was embarrassed to admit to the fact.

What would it matter if he had been?

Surely the measure of a man had more to do with the way his parents raised him than the street upon which they lived at the time of his birth. Wasn't it possible to come from dire circumstances and still make a good life? Or was this one time when Evelyn's antiquated notions about class and breeding held merit?

The thought triggered another, far more interesting one: where had Garrison Black hailed from, specifically? Quite possibly very close to where Rosemary now stood. Here was where much of the criminal element originated, and even though it was made up of several neighborhoods, they tended to get lumped under the umbrella of the East End.

Had Black been from Mayfair, for instance, it would have made much better fodder for the papers. More money, after all, meant a much bigger scandal; Arabelle had lived in Mayfair—not all that far from Rosemary's neighborhood in Marylebone—and her story had been splashed all over the front pages.

She wasn't the only one with Garrison Black on the brain, it seemed, a fact that was brought to her attention when she overheard the end of a conversation between Hadley and Maddy.

"I can't speak with you when you're in this sort of mood." Maddy half-whispered, "Garrison Black. Garrison Black. Garrison Black. You know what, Hadley? If a madman murdered a blond woman within a quarter-mile of *my* house, I'd cover every inch of my hair with bootblack and be happy when someone did him in, so I didn't have to worry anymore."

As Rosemary had been in that exact position even before Black turned his attention on her, she agreed with Maddy.

"You understand nothing," Hadley growled.

It sounded like Hadley was in a right foul mood.

CHAPTER SEVENTEEN

Rosemary found Max sitting on her front stoop when she arrived home quite a bit later than she'd originally planned. Evidently, the staff had listened to Rosemary's instructions and taken the day off, locking the house up tightly on their way out.

"I'm so sorry," she apologized quickly, rushing up the steps. "Did I miss Freddie and Vera?"

"We're to meet them at the restaurant in an hour," Max said in a softer tone than she'd heard him use for quite a long while. "What on earth have you been up to?" he asked then, taking in her disheveled appearance and reddened hands. There was no judgment, only curiosity, and Rosemary's spirits soared.

She smiled and said, "I'll explain later. Just let me nip upstairs and change. I won't be but a moment."

Max caught her hand and held it in his for a pointed, poignant moment, pulling her towards him gently. Her breath caught in her throat as he leaned in for one short kiss that spoke a thousand words. It was an apology, a promise to start fresh, and not caring to know what had prompted such, Rosemary returned it in kind.

"I'll wait," he said as he let her go, "as long as you need."

She tripped up the stairs to her rooms with a lightness she hadn't felt in days and did exactly as she'd promised: made short work of cleaning up and making herself presentable. A mere handful of minutes later, she returned to the sitting room where Max sat sipping a glass of gin he'd lifted from the drinks cart. Rosemary looked fresher than anyone ought to, in his estimation, after such a short time.

That evening, they stayed far away from Kettner's. Rosemary feared she might never return to the champagne bar after the ordeal with the mugger in the alley, but dinner was delicious all the same.

Vera raised her glass just as the pudding was served and toasted, in her southern American drawl, "I want to thank Rosemary for being my inspiration. Without you, love, I would never have been cast as the lead role in this play."

Frederick winked at his sister as he clinked his glass and beamed with adoration towards his wife. "It was your talent, Vera, my dear, above all else. Take your credit where it's due."

Rosemary resisted the urge to blow a raspberry in his

direction but couldn't hold back a smile. Frederick had had that effect on her for as long as she could remember.

When Max watched her from across the table, his eyes soft, she felt as though she hadn't a care in the world. When he held her close on the dance floor of the jazz club after dinner, Rosemary floated on air. And when his fingers entwined with hers during the walk back towards Park Road, she truly believed the worst was behind them. Even Vera's insistence on copying her every move couldn't penetrate the happy fog.

What she saw on her doorstep upon arriving home turned everything upside down. What—or rather, who—was sprawled across the landing made Rosemary's stomach drop clear to the ground.

"Bloody hell, Des. Is that you?" Frederick broke free from Vera's side and rushed ahead. "What in the devil are you doing here?"

Desmond Cooper raised himself off the landing and met his friend halfway up the steps. He and Frederick clapped one another on the back, their smiles both miles wide. Desmond's eyes quickly flicked to Rosemary, and he wiggled his brows in a gesture that brought a wide grin to her face and an immediate scowl to Max's.

"This has to be some sort of twisted joke." Vera stepped back, arms akimbo, and glared at Desmond with mock-hatred. "You're meant to be in America, Cooper, with the love of your life, remember? Or did she realize what a rotter you are and throw you over for a more handsome man?"

Pain crossed Desmond's face, and he swallowed hard. "Actually, Vera, Amelia did throw me over, and she *was* the love of my life," he said, and for a long moment, the air grew very still as Vera realized she may have gone too far.

Then Desmond roared with laughter, and Vera looked as though she might strangle him with her bare hands. "You're such an easy mark, Vera *Woolridge*!" Desmond said, skipping down the steps to kiss her cheek.

she swatted him away, but couldn't keep herself from smiling.

Desmond turned next to Rosemary, took her hand, and brought it to his lips, his eyes never leaving hers. Max stood watching, his nostrils flaring even wider than before until Desmond finished making his rounds.

"Inspector," Desmond drew himself up tall, his tone overly formal even while his eyes sparkled mischievously, and saluted Max.

"Mr. Cooper," Max replied even more tightly, a warning in his voice that Desmond duly ignored. In fact, he seemed to find amusement in the whole ordeal, even winking at Rosemary as he turned back to his oldest friend, Frederick.

When Desmond was around, the four became as children again—miscreants in cahoots and on a search for trouble. It hadn't been hard to find and even less difficult to conceal from their parents—particularly when combined with Rosemary's creative imagination and Vera's talent for subterfuge.

As such, the group could spend days telling fantastical stories that both amused and somewhat alienated anyone outside their circle, including Max in particular. Something told him it was, at least a little bit, that way by design.

This wasn't Max's first brush with the charismatic Desmond Cooper, but he thought the problem—specifically the concern over Desmond's interest in Rosemary—had been solved by Amelia, the attractive nanny to whom Vera referred. However, it seemed Desmond had gotten the brush off and was now sniffing around where he no longer belonged: Rosemary's skirts.

Max tried to calm his nerves. After all, he trusted her implicitly, at least with regards to romantic overtures. Rosemary might keep secrets when it came to her investigations, but wouldn't do anything to break his heart, that Max knew. Trouble, however, tended to follow Desmond everywhere he went, almost as unrelentingly as it stalked Rosemary. Additionally, to Max's discomfort, Desmond also shared with Rosemary a nearly absurd lack of concern regarding self-preservation. The two of them together was a recipe for disaster.

At least Garrison Black was out of the picture, for that Max was even more grateful now than ever before.

Rosemary watched while the two men engaged in an utterly absurd silent struggle of egos, herself fluctuating between true irritation and rueful exasperation. They behaved as if she were the wishbone torn out of a turkey carcass, trying to see who could yank the hardest and come away with the biggest piece.

She couldn't blame Max for his annoyance, but Rosemary still found herself thrilled to pieces that good old Desmond was back again. Admittedly, for years she'd carried a schoolgirl torch for him, but she'd chosen Max before Desmond ran off with Amelia, and Rosemary regretted nothing.

They'd shared one kiss, she and Desmond, some time ago in Cyprus—a kiss that should have been a dream come true—but instead, served to show Rosemary exactly where her heart belonged. Choosing Max, however, didn't mean she no longer cared about Desmond. The bottom line was that he lightened the mood and, considering the emotional rain and drear she'd been forced to endure recently, *light* was something Rosemary desperately wanted to feel.

"Seriously, Des," she pressed, "we're thrilled to see you," though, perhaps she oughtn't to have spoken for Max, "but last we knew, you were on another continent!"

Desmond ran his fingers through his hair, now so long it flopped over his right eye in a rakish, devil may care fashion. "Why don't we have a private wingding while I tell you all about my adventure into mystery over a nightcap?" he suggested, nodding his head towards the front door. "Some of the good stuff you've hidden in the back of the drinks cupboard, perhaps?"

"Why does everyone always think I'm holding out?" Rosemary wanted to know.

Vera snorted and deadpanned, "Because you *are*, dear."

"Max, what do you say?" Rosemary turned to him, torn between hoping he'd join them and wishing he would make the rest of the evening easier on her and just return to his flat.

Had things not been strained between the two of them recently, or had he been a lesser man, Max might have agreed to stay and take part in the verbal sparring match that would, no doubt, occur between himself and Desmond. But despite what he thought of Desmond, Max *was* the bigger man—a man who wouldn't stoop to the level of childish antics. Instead, he took the high road.

"I've an early shift tomorrow, and you'll all have a lot of catching up to do." Rosemary was relieved not only for the reprieve but at the knowledge that he still trusted her despite the recent friction between them.

He bade his goodbye, stooping slightly—just enough to pierce his nemesis with one more glare that spoke volumes but ultimately did nothing to dampen Desmond's spirits.

Chapter Eighteen

Desmond flopped into one of the sitting room chairs and accepted the drink—mixed with the good stuff, of course—Frederick handed him.

"I wish I could say I returned to valiantly save our Rosie here from a mass murderer, but there isn't a steamship in the world that could have sailed the Atlantic in just three days, so I won't try to pretend. It's true, Amelia and I parted ways. Amicably, of course," he continued until Frederick interrupted.

"When is it ever anything but amicable with you, Des?" Frederick leaned back in his chair, crossed his legs, and took a sip of his cocktail, all the while grinning like the Cheshire cat. Their friendship was based on a solid foundation of good-natured ribbing, and they'd months of it to make up for. "The dames practically thank you while they pack their bags. I don't know how you do it."

With a twinkle in his eye, Desmond winked at Vera.

"Up until quite recently, Freddie boy, you held the crown on that count. I learned everything I know from you!"

"Desmond, darling," Vera replied with an arched brow, "you're giving my husband far too much credit—yourself, as well, for that matter. These dames, as you so charmingly say, simply knew when to cut their losses and make a clean exit."

A mix of subtle and blatant but always affectionate digs passed between the foursome like a hot potato, the type of verbal sparring only the oldest of friends can achieve without resorting to fisticuffs. It filled the sitting room with laughter and an ease that had been mostly absent for the last several months.

"Do you want to hear the story or not?" Desmond asked with a pointed snarl in Vera's direction. He shifted in his seat, switched legs, and lit a cigarette. Then he arched one eyebrow and waited a beat before continuing.

"Well, you see, it was a balmy summer night...." Desmond's voice turned mock-serious, causing Frederick to pick up a cushion from the sofa next to him and heave it at his friend's head.

Desmond ducked, deftly, and raised his hands in surrender. "All right, I'll tell it straight. Amelia left me for another man, but her departure was a blessing in disguise. She was far too much of a bluenose for me, I discovered. Positively no sense of humor whatsoever!"

"Enough to take up with the likes of you." Vera toasted Desmond from her spot next to Frederick.

Frederick, in turn, toasted her. "Good one, darling."

Ignoring them both, Desmond continued, "We both knew what would happen before we even got off the boat, but we pretended for a few weeks, and then I woke one morning to find a note. She'd run off with an accountant, of all people! According to the letter, he wasn't even terribly good-looking, either, just more stable than me. And that was that—a relief, to be certain. That's also just about when my trip started to get interesting. Unfortunately, the whole thing was cut short. You see, the old girl finally bought it." Desmond remained stoic, but his voice rose an octave, and he was forced to clear his throat.

For several years Desmond had acted as companion to his ailing, elderly, and very wealthy aunt. When concerns arose regarding contents of her will, he'd been tasked with ensuring the vast sum of money remained where it belonged—with the Cooper family.

Somehow, though, in the course of things, Desmond had come to realize he was truly fond of her—far fonder than the rest of the family. As far as he was concerned, they were a wake of vultures, all poised to descend and make off with their respective pieces of the pie before the body was even cold.

"Part of me hopes she left it all to the nuns. I can just imagine the look on my jingle-brained cousins' faces—it would be priceless. We won't find out until the official reading, and that's not to take place until after the funeral."

"To the old girl. May she rest in peace." Frederick would toast nearly anything, but he'd spent some time with Desmond's aunt during their misspent youth, and carried a fondness for the old girl, as well.

"Auntie." The other three returned the toast, and drank to her heavenly passage.

The niceties observed, Desmond continued, "But now, I'm a vagabond, unless, of course, one of you takes pity on me. I can't stand the thought of holing up with Mother and Father. Not right now, anyway. They'll undoubtedly want to grill me for details about the will, and those, quite honestly, are just as much a mystery to me as to them—not that they'd believe me if I told them that."

Of course, Rosemary extended the hospitable offer. "You're welcome to stay in the guest room upstairs if you like," she said, certain Max would be less than thrilled about the arrangement. He was right in assessing that Desmond wasn't exactly desperate for funds; and could, in fact, more than afford the most lavish suite at any one of London's top hotels. However, being a sociable sort, Desmond preferred a friendly bed to one with room service.

"I think I'd prefer your guest room to the prospect of bunking with the newlyweds," he said, hooking his thumb in Frederick and Vera's direction. "Although, they seem rather tame, don't they, all things considered? How's being manacled working for you, Freddie? Beginning to chafe yet?"

"Manacled?" Rosemary frowned.

"Shackled. Ball and chain. Lot of names for the same thing in the states," Desmond offered a cheeky smile and tapped his finger where a wedding ring might rest.

Frederick smiled languidly from his perch on the sofa, where Vera lounged with her legs in his lap. Between sips of his G&T, he rubbed one of her feet casually, and Rosemary was thrilled to see he looked happier than a pig in mud.

"You only wish you had what I do," Frederick replied with a wink.

They both knew he was right, but Desmond wasn't one to concede his point so easily. "I seem to recall," he said, smug now, "a time when you abhorred the thought of settling down. It wasn't so long ago either, mate, although I can't say I'm surprised. You always did have a *soft spot* for our resident thespian." Desmond crossed his legs and sat back in his chair, watching merrily as Frederick's expression darkened.

"Tread carefully, Des old boy," Frederick warned. His

wife's eyes narrowed dangerously in reply, while Desmond merely appeared to be enjoying himself immensely.

"Why does your friend look like the cat who ate the canary?" Vera demanded.

Frederick slugged back the rest of his drink and raised an eyebrow. "I suppose he's referring to the Easter scavenger hunt at Woolridge House that you—ahem—won."

Vera's nostrils flared, and Rosemary leaned forward. When her brother and Vera got after one another, it was better than a front-row seat at a prizefight.

"What are you saying, *husband*?" Her tone made it sound as though the title could be revoked at any moment. She pushed him away with her feet and stood, her arms crossed as she stared him down.

By now, Frederick had resigned himself to his fate and, in perfect Frederick fashion, decided if he was in for a penny, he might as well be in for a pound. "You see, my love, the thing is...you didn't so much win as I *let* you win. It's a mere matter of semantics, really."

"Semantics?" Vera fired back, her eyes sparkling with righteous indignation. Two circles of pink rose to her cheeks, and she looked like she could spit fire if she wanted to.

Frederick shifted in his chair and winked at his wife. "Perhaps I let you win because, deep down, I knew I was mad for you, darling. It was years ago; nothing to get all hot and bothered over now."

"You only wish I was *hot and bothered*, Frederick Woolridge," Vera said languidly, sinking back down onto the settee on the other side of the coffee table, next to Rosemary. "And your desperate attempts to placate me really are beneath you, *darling*."

Desmond took the opportunity to lob the cushion back across the room, hitting Frederick squarely in the face.

Later, after Vera and Frederick had gone home, Desmond turned to Rosemary and asked, "How are you really getting on, Rosie? This whole thing must be dreadful for you, given what you've already been through."

Truly, she'd grown quite tired of hearing that particular phrase; ask any widow, she's sure to agree. And yet, she'd also grown adept at letting the irritation roll off her back.

"You know me, I'm getting on well enough, mostly thanks to those two, although I will say they can be positively sickening," Rosemary replied lightly. Her eyes took on a far-off expression and became rooted to one spot on the wall.

Desmond turned, tried to follow her gaze, but then he realized she was staring at something only she could see—something from her past, no doubt. "You've always been tough, Rose. Even when we were kids, you'd jump off the highest branch of the tree—in a skirt, no less—skin your knee, and keep right on going."

Rosemary smiled at the memory. "That wasn't me. It was Vera, in that red dress she wore everywhere until it was full of holes and my mother had to call hers," she rambled, slightly tipsy. "I've thought about that dress often over the years. It represented everything I loved about Vera; her free spirit and her disregard for order and compliance. All the things she was what I could never be. But she didn't get to keep it, did she? Because it wasn't proper. Well, *life* isn't proper, and it's certainly not any fun being of the dress-wearing gender, I can assure you," Rosemary said, shaking her head and coming out of her reverie.

"I'm thrilled you're back, Desmond dear, but I'm positively knackered," she begged off, heading for the stairs and the sanctuary of her bed. "Make yourself at home."

Chapter Nineteen

Miss Rose, please, there's no need for you to muck about in the dirt," Vera overheard the comment from the voice of a man she didn't recognize but assumed to be one of the crew working on Rosemary's garden redo.

When she turned the corner around a large arborvitae shrub, her suspicion was confirmed. A man wearing a pair of overalls and an exasperated expression looked down on her friend who unabashedly mucked about in the dirt, as he had so eloquently phrased it.

A smile spread across Vera's face even as she directed a sour, narrow-eyed glare in the man's direction.

Rosemary, to her credit, brushed off the remark. "Thank you for your concern, but I'm quite content here," she said pointedly, to which the workman shrugged, rolled his eyes, and sauntered away across the lawn.

Vera bade Rosemary good morning and plunked herself down on a flat boulder conveniently placed on the other side of the path.

"You're raising quite the controversy, aren't you, Rosie?" Vera said sarcastically. "Deigning to kneel in your own garden! Don't you know you can pay people for that?"

Rosemary giggled. "Your impression of my mother is uncanny! You could scare the living daylights out of Frederick with it."

The thought caused Vera to blanch. "One might think these men would be grateful for the reprieve," she commented.

"They don't want to feel superfluous, is all," Rosemary said, continuing her quest to arrange the mulch beneath the rhododendrons into a neat, attractive hump. "They're being paid to do a job, and their pride takes a hit every time I cross a task off their list. I'll be grateful when they've finished the stonework; it's all that's left, and then they'll pack up and leave us to our own devices."

"You won't have a gardener at all?" Vera asked, surprised.

Rosemary shook her head. "Wadsworth thinks I'm addled, but Gladys and Anna agreed to lend a hand, and Ariadne has assured me we're more than capable of tending a garden this small."

Wanting to argue the point, Vera realized she'd boxed herself neatly into a corner. She couldn't very well claim

Rosemary fully capable, make a joke about hiring help, and then in the next breath insinuate she couldn't manage on her own!

To be safe, Vera merely changed the subject. "Surely you're almost finished. Fancy a trip to the shops? I need to browse the windows; take a look at some of the American imports. You know, really get a feel for how my character might dress."

"The grass is always greener, isn't it?" Rosemary replied wryly. "All those American ladies looking for European imports, and here you've got your pick and would prefer the opposite." Not that Vera wouldn't look smashing in the latest American fashions; she could wrap herself in freshly wrinkled burlap, toss on a few accessories, and end up looking chic.

"Do you want to come or not?" Vera jabbed at Rosemary with her elbow in a gesture repeated so often over the years of their friendship it had become a habit. "Looking authentic might give me the edge I need to steal the show from that creepy, notebook-toting Cora."

"Notebook-toting? What an odd turn of phrase. Is that American?"

Vera shrugged. "She carries that thing everywhere, and she's always scribbling in it. I just know she's writing scathing things about me, and I want to know what they are."

At times, Vera could be quite exhausting. "You can't

know that," Rosemary countered. "She could be writing any number of notes that have nothing to do with you."

"I heard her talking with that nice chap who got the part of the victim's brother during our last rehearsal, and he told her she should have been cast as the lead." By her attempt and failure to maintain an even tone, Rosemary knew overhearing the comment stung Vera's pride.

"Because a nice young man would never use such blatant flattery to turn a woman's head," Rosemary pointed out the flaw in Vera's thinking. "What did she have to say for herself?"

Vera sniffed, and injected a breathless quality into her voice. "The best actors treat every part as if it were the lead." In her normal range Vera continued. "Isn't that utter nonsense?"

Now, Rosemary couldn't hold back a laugh. "Vera Woolridge, you really are the living end."

"Why?" Vera asked, miffed.

"She's quoting you, you silly thing," Rosemary said with a roll of her eyes. "From an article in the paper after your first starring role."

Having the good sense to look chastened, Vera dithered for a moment before saying, "Be that as it may, I still believe she hates me, and the only thing that will soothe my wounded pride is a day in the shops. Will you indulge me, Rosie dear?"

Rosemary stood and brushed the dirt from her knees. "If you'll drop the theater talk for the rest of the day, then yes, I'll accompany you, just as soon as I've put these things away and changed my clothes." With that, she headed for the potting shed with a bucket, a pair of gloves, and her trusty soil cultivator, but when she opened the door, Rosemary dropped everything and let out a screech that sent the crows flying for the safety of their nest. "Eeeeek!"

"Miss Rose!" A voice thundered from across the garden, and in a flash, Jack appeared next to Vera, still holding the shovel he'd been using to dig the trench on the other side of the lawn.

A laugh bubbled up in Rosemary's throat. "It was just a mouse," she explained. "I don't know why I screamed. He's actually quite adorable." She pointed to the floor just inside the door where a little mouse (Vera wasn't sure if she'd call it *adorable!*) stood on his hind legs and glanced about nervously. Its tiny nose twitched, and it peered up at Rosemary with curiosity.

Out of nowhere, Jack's shovel came down on top of the critter with a thud that caused both women to jump nearly out of their skin. Rosemary's eyes widened, and her hand came up to cover her mouth.

"S—sorry, Miss—Miss Rose," Jack stuttered nervously. "They're rodents, and the boss says we can't leave even one. There's always another, waiting to take its place."

He lifted the shovel to reveal the body of the poor mouse, and, rodent or not, Rosemary couldn't help but feel sorry it had been dispatched in such a manner. Was it better than being drowned in a cage? She decided neither was a desirable way to go and that she'd had enough of the garden for one afternoon.

"Perhaps you should have gotten a cat, Rosie, instead of a dog," Vera commented, her eyes still fixed on the tiny corpse.

"Not to worry, Miss Vera," came Wadsworth's voice. He had, evidently, approached from behind, and he sounded amused. "I'll take care of any pests that invade the garden, at least until our mistress decides she's had her fill of trudging about and rehires the gardener."

Vera very nearly choked on a breath, and Rosemary wound up a retort that never left her lips, for something more interesting caught her eye across the lawn. She could have sworn she saw Abigail Redberry lurking about on the other side of the hedge. In fact, she was positive she'd seen her neighbor—and supposed friend's—eyes peeking through the foliage. Before Rosemary had a chance to say anything, the figure turned and beat a hasty retreat away from the fence.

"What was that about?" Vera asked sharply. "Abigail is usually quite chatty—sometimes irritatingly so, so why is she avoiding us? Do we have egg on our faces or something?"

Rosemary forced her gaze away from the fence and turned to Vera. "Metaphorically speaking, I believe we do. What really irks is that it was a coup to live next to a *lady detective*," Rosemary put emphasis on the term and rolled her eyes skyward, "when it was Abigail's husband—the supposed *Killer Dentist of Park Road*—slated for the gallows. Now, I feel like a leper. Perhaps I was on the right track in considering moving to a new neighborhood."

"Oh, Rosie, to hell with her, then. She's obviously a fair-weather friend, so good riddance. Everyone who matters knows the truth. Besides, you can't move now that Freddie and I live around the corner!"

"What everyone knows is what the papers are spouting," Rosemary replied, ignoring the last bit, her eyes drawn back to where Abigail had disappeared. "You don't think…" she trailed off, shaking her head to divest herself of the notion.

Vera's eyes narrowed, and she spat, "It might have been Abigail who called the papers. Is that what you're thinking? Did you tell her about the death threat?"

Rosemary nodded. "I did. I thought the Redberrys deserved to know a murderer was watching the house next door. I urged them to take caution, and they assured me they would keep the information to themselves."

"And you think maybe Abigail didn't," Vera

suggested. "I thought better of her than that, but it would explain the odd behavior."

For a moment, Rosemary stewed over the notion, but finally, she shook her head and renewed her focus on Vera, whose allegiance she'd never in a thousand years have cause to question. "Suddenly, I feel quite pleased to join you at the shops."

The pair linked arms and had made it almost to the terrace when Rosemary's face fell. "Wonderful," she muttered sarcastically at the sight of a familiar, huddled figure making her way across the terrace behind Wadsworth.

"Who's that?" Vera asked, still out of earshot.

"Just another thorn trying to work its way into my side is all," Rosemary explained and then plastered a smile on her face. "Miss Keller, hello," she said. "Is there something I can do for you? We were just on our way out."

"Oh, goodness me, I seem to have arrived at the most inopportune moment, haven't I?" Briony Keller offered a pseudo-apology.

Rosemary had thought her hint regarding her afternoon plans might have discouraged the question, but she should have known better. "Could I trouble you for a word, Mrs. Lillywhite? I've tried reaching you over the telephone, but it seems you've been indisposed."

Miss Keller pierced Wadsworth with a knowing look.

"Of course, I can spare a moment," Rosemary said politely, keeping her thoughts from coloring her voice or showing on her face. "But only one."

After the morning's paper, in which she wasn't, for the first time in a week, accused of having anything to do with Garrison Black's death, she had hoped the fanfare surrounding her discovery of his body might be winding down. Rosemary further hoped that perhaps along with it might go the incessant telephone calls, the postal deluge, and the unexpected visitors, but unfortunately, that didn't seem to be the case after all.

"Apologies, my lady," Wadsworth said. "I attempted to inform Miss Keller that you were unavailable, but she insisted it's a matter of the utmost importance."

With a nod, Rosemary absolved her butler of blame. "It's quite all right, Wadsworth. You did the right thing." She dismissed him and turned to her guest, earning Vera's admiration and, she feared as she caught the expression in her friend's eyes, another round of the mirror game. "What can I do for you, Miss Keller? My schedule is just as full as it was the last time you called."

If she'd thought the woman had returned to beg for her help with the threatening letters, Rosemary was mistaken.

"Oh, dear heavens, no. That's not why I'm here. You

see, I've lost something—something of great importance to me, and I thought I might have lost it here. I don't suppose you've found a gold locket, have you?"

Hope colored Miss Keller's face, plain as day. She was a woman of modest means, that Rosemary had already surmised, but also a prideful one. The locket must have meant quite a lot to her if she was willing to come all the way back and risk being turned away, and Rosemary did have a heart.

"I'm sorry," she said, shaking her head and wishing she had a different answer, "I haven't."

Miss Keller's eyes shifted to where the wheelbarrow rested. "What about one of them? Do you suppose they'd hand something like that over if they did find it?"

Rosemary's eyes whipped over to where the landscapers were busy finishing up with the stonework. She didn't want to admit it, but what Miss Keller suggested wasn't out of the realm of possibility. How well did she know these men? Not well at all.

"I will search the grounds, and I will most certainly speak to the landscapers," Rosemary promised. When Miss Keller looked at her expectantly, she added, "in private. Please, leave your contact information, and if I find the locket, I'll make sure it gets returned to you."

The woman could hardly argue, though Rosemary suspected she'd have fancied a thorough look around the garden herself had she been given the opportunity. Instead, she followed Rosemary and Vera out through the front door, which Wadsworth deliberately locked up tightly behind them.

Chapter Twenty

Several hours later than planned, Rosemary arrived back at home with a car boot full of packages. She'd often wondered why Vera insisted shopping could cure most of life's woes but found that just this once she understood the phenomenon completely. Anna nearly swooned over a particularly fetching dress in a floral pastel print before scurrying off for another date with her young constable.

"He's treating you well, yes?" Rosemary asked, a warning tone in her voice that suggested if he wasn't, he'd be in a world of trouble from several angles.

Flushing scarlet, Anna replied, "Oh, yes, he's a gentleman all right. A perfect gentleman." Something about her tone made Rosemary wonder if Anna wished he wasn't, quite. "Perhaps he only wants to be friends," Anna mused before taking her leave, letting Rosemary know she'd been correct in her estimation.

At least, Rosemary thought, it sounded as though poor

Constable Clayton hadn't much experience with the young ladies, and that suited her just fine. Anna was a good girl, and she deserved only the best.

With Desmond attending to family business, Rosemary found herself alone for the evening, and so she decided she was ready to clear the downstairs office cum studio of everything related to her investigation into Garrison Black.

It was time to put the past behind her, and Rosemary felt that only then would she be able to decide how she wanted to proceed with regard to her *lady detective* status. Oh, how she hated that phrase now that she'd seen it splashed in newsprint, the contrary component of her personality almost making her want to embrace rather than reject it, on principle alone.

Quickly, Rosemary pulled the boards holding all her Black research into the center of the room. She plucked the push pins one by one and set each newspaper clipping, photograph, and case note on the desk that used to be Andrew's.

She'd yet to decide if she wanted to keep the desk or not. It, along with the plaque emblazoned with her name and would-be title, had become entwined symbols of her indecision regarding her way forward in life.

Rosemary could easily settle back down, get married, and continue on in the same direction she'd been headed when she became a widow. Or, she could blaze a new trail of her own and officially accept the mantle of private investigator. Had he lived, she'd have willingly followed Andrew down a similar path, albeit riding on his coattails rather than leading the charge.

Was she only holding onto the possibility because that was what *he* had wanted? The answer was that Rosemary wasn't certain. Her grief had become tangled with the notion, and now, she felt pressured to make a choice. Except, it was her choice and hers alone; she was the one applying the pressure.

Rosemary sighed and sat down, suddenly tired, and decided it wasn't a decision she needed to make right away. She fingered one of the newspaper clippings, noting sadly just how many headlines had featured Garrison Black over the previous decade, and picked up the most faded of the lot.

It was an article from near the middle of Black's reign of terror, dated six years prior, and served as a warning to the flaxen-haired ladies of London. The streets were no longer safe; the person who had committed three similar murders four years before had returned and killed again.

Rosemary glanced over to the journal she'd received from Esme at the last LLV meeting. It, too, was from nearly six years before. She checked the dates and calculated it was written after the newspaper article but prior to the death of Constable Benton Greene and

Black's subsequent disappearance.

She opened the journal and began to read. Rather than the dry, meticulous recounting of his official reports, here, Prescott had recorded his own fears and frustrations related to the case.

> *If we could only uncover the truth about Black's past, I believe we could discern his motivation and perhaps even parlay that knowledge into a successful capture. He's obviously highly intelligent; his murders are well-planned, and he has, so far, successfully evaded all our efforts to track him down.*
>
> *The commissioner suspects Black has an accomplice; however, I firmly disagree. Even if he found someone as twisted as he is, he'd never extend the level of trust it would take to collaborate. No, I don't agree that Black may have a partner.*
>
> *I do hope and have to believe there's someone out there with the information I need. Perhaps the same someone who called in the anonymous tip leading us to Black's identity in the first place.*

Now that was news to Rosemary. She'd never heard tell of an anonymous tip, and the thought struck her as ironic considering it was, also, what had sold her to the press and made her life miserable ever since she'd discovered Black's body on her doorstep. She decided ruminating about it wouldn't change anything and shook the thought from her mind.

With a start, Rosemary realized she didn't actually know much about the early days of the Black investigation. What evidence had pointed to him as the murderer and prompted the manhunt so many years ago?

None of the answers were mentioned in the more recent articles. The case had become sensationalized, containing fewer facts and more conjecture the longer it went on. Might there be other facts hidden in those early pieces? Facts that would, by now, be considered 'old news', and yet might provide some clue to Black's motives? Rosemary couldn't articulate why she cared other than to justify that it was a mystery—a mystery being something she simply couldn't abide.

Intrigued, she pinned the article back up on the corkboard, then returned to the stack of notes and clippings, searching for the oldest of the bunch. For two solid hours, Rosemary moved between the desk and the boards, and when she was done, she'd managed to lay out Black's criminal career in chronological order.

Ten years before, three women were brutally murdered, the police quite unable to pinpoint the killer's identity. Then, as Prescott's journal stated, an anonymous tip revealed Garrison Black's involvement. Irrefutable evidence tied him to the murders, and from then on, he'd been the most wanted man in London.

Yet, Black continued to evade capture, beginning a second spree of murders four years after the first. Except, this time, he didn't cover his tracks well enough. Prescott's team bore down and finally had Black cornered, but they didn't know he'd taken a hostage, and they weren't prepared. A young constable named Benton Greene got caught in the crossfire, and Black escaped once more.

Prescott continued, funneling all his energy into finding Black, and finally, his perseverance paid off. All seemed well; a murderer was behind bars, awaiting a trial that would surely lead to his execution. But then, aided by someone—a corrupt constable, or perhaps a warden—Black escaped! Whoever had betrayed the constabulary was Max's problem now, and despite what she'd said during their fight, Rosemary believed he would solve it.

Rosemary reread the journal one more time. She happened to agree with Sergeant Prescott's theory; it only made sense that Black worked alone. It only made sense his death was a happy accident and not perpetrated by someone who might still be out there, stalking her in the night.

But then, what about the tip? Where had it come from, and what was the connection between Black and the person who left it? Rosemary sat back in her chair, deep in thought.

Garrison Black had come from modest beginnings; that much was stated clearly in the case files. That he'd had a difficult childhood was also no secret: abused by his mother, thrown over by his father, and ridiculed in school, according to the notes.

Her curiosity fully piqued, Rosemary began a targeted search back through the documents. Which school was the site of Black's tormented youth? What neighborhood had he hailed from? Somewhere in the East End, she imagined, possibly quite near where the homeless ex-Tommies now lived. How many of them had returned to the familiar streets of their youth?

Perhaps Garrison Black had done the same.

After a few moments, Rosemary found the piece of information she was looking for and, satisfied, made a note on a pad of paper from the top desk drawer and then stopped short.

Had Max been right? Was she really unable to control herself? The thought followed her around for the rest of the evening like a hard little pebble in the bottom of her shoe.

Chapter Twenty-One

The next morning Rosemary awakened with purpose. She had decided, sometime in the middle of the night, that she wouldn't be able to rest until she'd satisfied her curiosity and at least checked into Black's past. If it seemed at all ironic that she had worked her way back around to investigating despite being desperate to call the case closed and walk away, Rosemary pretended not to notice.

Nobody who knew her would have been surprised, which is why Desmond didn't even raise an eyebrow when she informed him she required his assistance. They were in the back garden, Desmond being the only person who hadn't responded with skepticism when she explained her desire to make friends with the crows.

"They're smarter than they look," was all he said, though truth be told, their beady little eyes always made him feel as though he were being watched, judged, and found wanting. It was more than disconcerting, but he seemed to understand Rosemary's fascination, for which she was grateful. The next person who pursed their lips disapprovingly might earn themselves a thorough tongue lashing.

"Let me see if I understand," Desmond said after the crows had finished eating and, mercifully, returned to their nest in the church steeple. "You want me to follow you into the worst part of the city in search of information about a mass murderer who wanted nothing more than to break into your home, torture, and kill you? You haven't told anyone where we're going, and you've been expressly told by your beau, a chief inspector of the London police, to keep a wide berth when it comes to Garrison Black. And there's no reason whatsoever for any of this because the man is dead and was, in fact, found that way on your own doorstep."

"That essentially sums it up," Rosemary said languidly. "Are you in, or are you out?"

Desmond shrugged. "Do you really have to ask? Of course, I'm in, and not only because you're sure to find yourself in a heap of trouble without me, but also because I believe my recent experience with such means I can be of some assistance in the mystery-solving department."

Rosemary bit back a laugh, deciding she needed his help and therefore had better be polite. "I'm sure you'll be a great asset to this endeavor," she said seriously.

"I do have one condition, however," Desmond added. "I get to drive."

To that, Rosemary happily agreed. She gathered her hat, handbag, and the folder containing information she hoped would direct her to Garrison Black's last known residence.

"The exact address isn't listed in any of these notes, so we may be running a fool's errand, anyway," she said out loud.

Desmond glanced in her direction. "In all seriousness, what exactly are you hoping to find, Rose? He's dead and gone. Why go digging at all? Is this about the papers? You know the stories will blow over."

She considered the question for a moment before answering. "It's not about the press, at least not entirely. Freddie would probably call it my obstinate nature; Vera would cite morbid curiosity. Perhaps it's a little bit of both, but I suppose it feels too much like unfinished business. Do you know what I mean?"

His eyebrows drew together, and he glanced over at Rosemary with an enigmatic expression. "Yes, I believe I do," he said as if there might be something more he wanted to say but he let the subject drop. They rode the rest of the way to the East End, making companionable chitchat about Desmond's time in America while Rosemary consulted the map.

"You should plan a trip, Rose. It's something to see,

I'll tell you," Desmond promised.

Rosemary nodded, considering the possibility. She did enjoy seeing new places and meeting new people, and the stain from her recent trip to Cyprus—where she'd had to solve a murder case—had almost entirely dissipated.

"We're almost there," she realized with a start, all thoughts of steamships and cross-continental travel forgotten. Rosemary directed Desmond through the neighborhood of Whitechapel to the cross streets indicated in Sergeant Prescott's notes. She had checked each line of his journals and every newspaper article for a more specific address but to no avail.

Upon arriving, she couldn't tell whether or not luck was on her side. The intersection sat smack in the middle of what constituted a mostly residential area. Soot-black brick buildings dominated three of the four corners, the last reduced to a pile of rubble the city had declined to remove.

Two children, a boy and a girl wearing little more than rags stared at the shiny black car as Desmond pulled to a stop, their eyes filled with both interest and something else. It took Rosemary a moment to realize the something else was anticipation, and she started when the children approached the car and held their hands out expectantly.

She reached into her handbag and deposited a shilling

into each of their fingers. "Skinflint," the girl snorted to Rosemary's surprise. The boy rolled his eyes, and the pair walked away. Desmond couldn't help but laugh at Rosemary's shocked expression.

"You used to be a lot nicer to me, Des," she sulked.

Desmond grinned in reply. "Those were entirely different circumstances," he qualified. "Of course, I was nice to you when I was actively trying to court you, but since I've ceased to find you romantically desirable, there's no longer any need for me to play the role of knight in shining armor."

Her mouth dropped open momentarily, but she snapped it shut quickly.

"However," Desmond continued, "I find it rather interesting that you seem to miss my more charming attributes." He wiggled his eyebrows at her, which she duly ignored, and went back to surveying her surroundings while vowing to keep her purse strings closed for the rest of the afternoon.

Desmond stayed by her side, refusing the suggestion that they split up to investigate the three possible buildings. A small part of him hoped to discover Garrison Black's home had been the one that sat demolished. He would prefer Rosemary lay the whole thing to rest and let him take her back to Marylebone but ultimately sensed it was not to be.

His hopes were dashed entirely, and Rosemary's lifted

when the very first inquiry paid out. A Mr. Sneed, the proprietor of the ground-floor shaving parlor on one corner of the street, knew exactly which flat Black had lived in.

"Think you're the first to come gawk at the place that birthed a mass murderer?" he'd asked rudely before pointing to the block of flats across the way. The most disheveled of the lot, it looked as though it, too, might soon crumble into ruin. "Second floor, third to the right."

When asked whether there might still be anyone around who remembered Garrison Black, Mr. Sneed pierced Rosemary with a curious stare. "People who live here don't usually have another choice. They also don't take kindly to rich ladies poking their noses in where they don't belong."

"Is there anyone, or isn't there?" Rosemary pressed. "Please, it's important."

Mr. Sneed considered for a long moment and then finally capitulated. Even he could see she wouldn't back down until she got what she wanted. "It's the landlady you're looking for, old Mrs. Brighton, but I'll eat my hat if she agrees to speak with you."

Instead of firing back that she'd hold him to the promise, Rosemary merely thanked Mr. Sneed and followed Desmond out the door. Her stomach fluttered as she braved the dark, uninviting stairwell, glad she'd had the forethought to bring Desmond along. It continued to churn while she climbed and still hadn't settled by the time she stood in front of the indicated flat.

A week's worth of uncollected newspapers and leaflets littered the floor outside the door. Nobody had been home for some time, it seemed, nor had anyone attempted to clear the debris from the hallway. Here, apparently, people didn't interfere with their neighbors' affairs.

Rosemary truly hadn't known what she expected to happen when she decided to come poking around Black's old home. She'd been running on instinct, and now that she was there, she found herself at a complete loss. It was an ordinary door in an ordinary, if rather depressing, building.

She had almost decided to turn around and pull Desmond out to the car and back to Marylebone when a muffled click preceded by the snick of metal sliding against metal sounded from the other side of the hallway. Rosemary whirled around just in time to see a peephole cover snap back closed.

Undeterred, she approached the door and rapped on it softly. "Mrs. Brighton? Is that you? Can I speak with you for a moment, please?"

"What about?" a raspy voice answered.

Rosemary steeled herself against the inevitable

brushoff but stated her purpose nonetheless. "I'd like to ask you some questions regarding Garrison Black."

Mrs. Brighton harrumphed and then snapped, "You another journalist? I ain't got nothing to say, just like I told the last one who came knocking."

"I'm not a journalist," Rosemary replied. "I'm a victim—at least, I almost was. My name is Rosemary Lillywhite. Garrison Black died on my doorstep, and now the papers are dragging my name through the mud." If the truth didn't grant her access, she would be forced to admit she'd dragged Desmond on a fool's errand. "Please, I have questions that need answering, and I believe you can help me."

Mrs. Brighton opened the peephole again and peered out at Rosemary with suspicion. "Consider yourself lucky to have been saved at all. You're one of few. Off with you, now, and let the dead rest! That poor boy will answer for his sins just like we all will—at the hands of God and God alone!"

A chill traveled up Rosemary's spine. She recalled all the letters she'd received recently. Most were supportive or inquisitive, but some were quite different, indeed. A few of the letter writers seemed to doubt Black's guilt in the murders, or at the very least, believed he'd been denied a chance to defend himself.

Rosemary didn't believe for one second this elderly woman was responsible for the most concerning, hand-delivered note, nor did it seem likely she'd sent any of the posted ones. Had she penned the letters, it stood to reason Rosemary's arrival would have garnered a stronger reaction. Still, if Mrs. Brighton felt some form of sympathy for Black, perhaps there was another way to convince her to talk.

"I know Garrison Black lived a hard life," Rosemary choked out the words she knew to be true but didn't truly believe, "and I'm sorry for that. I know his mother beat him, and I know his father left. I also know he's not the only one who has ever been hurt or abandoned by a parent; it's not an excuse for murder."

As Rosemary had hoped, Mrs. Brighton became agitated. "I—I didn't—certainly didn't imply—" she sputtered.

Rosemary sensed she had made an error and was now poised to lose any chance at getting the elderly lady to talk. One wrong word and Mrs. Brighten would close up like a clam. She hesitated but fortunately, Desmond had a solution at the ready.

"Do you really want to die without ever having told your story, Mrs. Brighton?" he demanded, shocking Rosemary with his bluntness. "You're not going to be around much longer, let's face it, and once you're gone, there won't be anyone out there who knows the truth."

The peephole slid shut, and for a long moment filled with contemplative silence, Rosemary thought for sure they'd been dismissed. Then Mrs. Brighton unfastened the locks and opened the door. "Come inside," she said stiffly, waiting until Desmond and Rosemary had entered before locking the door back up behind them.

Inside wasn't nearly as dismal as the dingy hallway. The flat was clean and smelled faintly of lye soap. She didn't offer tea but motioned for Rosemary and Desmond to take a seat once formal introductions had been made.

Mrs. Brighton herself was withered and wizened, deep lines crisscrossing her forehead. The apron worn over a faded dress was nearly translucent with age and wear, and her misshapen slippers evidenced the painful bunions that plagued both of her feet.

"I did know the Black family," she explained when they'd settled into chairs in the small dining area. "This building belonged to my husband. He was the one who took care of the tenants." Her eyes went misty as she became caught up in a memory.

"The place was in marginally better condition back then, but Barty still had to fight for the rents every month. The Blacks were the worst; the father spent near every shilling he ever made on one gamble or another— cards, horses, sports—anything that might pay out. 'Course, most the time, it didn't, and it wasn't him who suffered for it, was it? No, it was the mother and the child. She took to the drink and was the meanest drunk

I've ever seen. The boy bore the brunt of her anger, especially after Mr. Black run off. A shame is what it was; a crying shame for that poor boy."

Rosemary wasn't sure how many more times she could hear the man who had terrorized London for the last decade be referred to with the level of affection with which Mrs. Brighton spoke. Beneath the table, she dug her fingernails into the palm of her hand until she was certain they'd left tiny half-moons embedded in the skin.

"He never trusted anyone, that boy. I tried to turn a blind eye, but it was impossible to ignore. He'd inherited his mother's mean streak—how could he not, with no other example? None of the neighborhood kids liked him. I think he frightened them, and they were right to be scared. Even as a child, his heart was just as black as his surname. He'd kick a puppy just as soon as pet it."

Mrs. Brighton grimaced, and Rosemary had to shake her head to divest herself of the image of someone hurting her precious little Dash.

"He simply didn't know how to love. Doesn't excuse what he did, mind, but Garrison Black was doomed from the start."

At that, Rosemary had to hold back a snort. She managed to do so, but only because she caught the look of warning Desmond shot in her direction.

"However," Mrs. Brighton explained, "it wasn't for lack of trying. Oh, yes, Gary did very much want to be loved, especially after Mrs. Black passed away. That was about twenty years ago now; he wasn't more than twenty himself then. I think he thought with her gone, he'd finally have a clean slate. Why he didn't immediately pack up and leave this place, I never understood. Finally, he seemed to find some happiness, but it didn't last. I'd hoped it would but knew it wouldn't. The girl—I never knew her name—looked too much like Mrs. Black for me to believe it a mere coincidence. Fair-haired, pretty, and with a sweet nature he would have tromped all over if given the chance."

"What happened to her?" Rosemary breathed. She was on the edge of her seat, a theory percolating. Could this mystery girl have become Black's first victim?

What Mrs. Brighton said next not only blew the thought from Rosemary's mind but set it reeling. "They had a row one night; a terrible row. About what, I couldn't tell you. Afterwards, he left—probably went on a bender. For all Garrison's fears, he'd turned out quite like his mother after all. Thank heavens Barty was here then. It was the only time I was ever scared of the boy. So, you can see why I wouldn't have told him that when she left, she was…in trouble." Mrs. Brighton's eyes widened meaningfully.

"You're saying this girl was pregnant with Garrison Black's child?" Rosemary could hardly believe what she was hearing, "a child he never knew existed?"

"What good would it have done to tell him?" she retorted. "If I'd ever regretted the decision, well, it was too late, wasn't it? I think whatever happened that night was the last straw. He returned for his belongings, paid up his rent, and disappeared. Later, when his name was splashed all over the papers, I wasn't surprised to discover what he'd done."

Rosemary sensed she'd learned all she could from Mrs. Brighton and found her ability to remain civil weaken even further. "How could you sit here all these years and watch while he terrorized people? Why didn't you tell your story to the police?"

Mrs. Brighton looked as though she thought Rosemary quite daft. "Perhaps you haven't noticed, but this ain't Mayfair. They'd have come, done nothing, and left me looking like a rat. What good do you think it would have done, girl? It wouldn't have changed anything."

"It might have saved lives—mine included!" Rosemary seethed. She wasn't sure exactly how but felt a conviction that, had the police known more about Garrison Black's background, they might have captured him sooner. "He was poised to enter my home, fully intent on murdering me!"

"You're still alive, aren't you?" Mrs. Brighton retorted. "You're not the kind of lady whose luck ever runs out. Your life is full of possibilities and opportunities. What would you know about the one Garrison Black was forced to lead? Nothing," she spat. "And now, I've said my piece, and it's time for you to go. Shoo, now, and don't come back!"

Rosemary's eyes lit on the pile outside the door to what was once Garrison Black's flat, and suddenly an inconceivable thought occurred to her: had he returned to his childhood home, and did just how far did Mrs. Brighton's sympathy extend? Far enough for her to be willing to welcome him back?

"Mrs. Brighton!" she exclaimed, whirling back around only to discover the landlady had already begun refastening the locks.

Rosemary looked at Desmond, eyes wide, and then was startled when the door opened, and a woman's voice shouted, "Keep it down out there!" followed by a spate of curse words that would have made a sailor blush.

The foul language rolled right off Rosemary's back. She felt only a great sense of relief, accompanied by the conviction that she could live, quite happily, without ever again returning to the East End of London.

Out loud, on the way back home, she declared, "I think I'll let Vera have her way with my hair; suddenly, I don't quite fancy being a blond anymore."

Chapter Twenty-Two

Before heading to the theater to fetch Vera from play rehearsal, Rosemary dropped Desmond off in front of the restaurant where he was slated to meet his family for tea. She intended to wait in the car while Vera finished up, but the afternoon had turned quite cool, and she found herself shivering against the upholstery.

The weather had been as changeable as a woman's mood for the past few days. To be properly prepared, Rosemary thought, one needed to wear a sleeveless dress but bring along an overcoat.

She got out of the car and fished around in the boot for the cardigan left there during the recent shopping trip, which she donned while listening intently to the voice wafting out from the open theater door. She retrieved her purse and wandered inside, where Vera held the stage, reciting a monologue Rosemary recognized from the script she'd been carrying around since returning from her honeymoon.

Riveted, Rosemary watched her friend, who no longer looked or sounded anything like her usual, lighthearted self. Indeed, she marveled, it was like looking in a mirror or, more accurately, what she thought it might be like to watch oneself on film. For Vera had adopted all of Rosemary's own mannerisms, from her posture to the way she tucked a stray lock of hair behind her ear, right down to the tone of Rosemary's voice. Other than the lines being delivered in an American accent, the resemblance was uncanny, somewhat unsettling, and entirely spellbinding.

When Vera finished, she stood and clapped, the sound ringing out across the auditorium at a higher volume than she'd intended. Vera looked up, and abruptly, she was herself again, waving merrily in Rosemary's direction.

"You were wonderful," Rosemary gushed when she'd met her friend at the foot of the stage.

Vera beamed, but her brow quickly wrinkled. "I'm still having trouble with the last half of the monologue, and it doesn't help to have Cora staring at me through narrowed eyes all the while I'm trying to perform."

She shivered exaggeratedly and pulled Rosemary into her dressing room. It wasn't much bigger than a broom cupboard, but it did have a vanity and chair on one side and on the other a small settee and a rack for clothes and accessories.

"There is most definitely something off about Cora, Rosie, and I'm not the only one who thinks so. She's developed quite the reputation in theater circles." Maybe Vera was getting worked up over nothing. Or maybe there was something odd about Cora. Either way, Vera wouldn't let it go until she dug out the whole story—and with Rosemary's help, whether offered or not.

"What's happened?" Giving in to the inevitable, Rosemary crossed her legs and leaned against the sofa back while Vera pulled out a crystal decanter and two glasses and poured them each a drink.

"Well," she said with a surreptitious look towards the door, "Reggie and Brenda—they play two of the red herrings—said Cora has quite the reputation." Vera paused for dramatic effect, but Rosemary indicated, with a twirl of her hand, to get on with the story.

"After some of your antics, I quite suspect she's not the only one," Rosemary said in dry tones.

"Fine, Rosie, sheesh. The moral of the story is: she's completely unhinged. Became obsessed with her last director. Started dropping off anonymous notes at his house—until, finally, his *wife*—" at that Vera raised a disapproving eyebrow, "had to run her off! She got fired, of course, and Brenda said she attacked another one of the actresses on her way out of the theater!"

"Maybe the other actress provoked her. You theater folk do tend towards passionate reactions."

That Cora's was a rather damning story, Rosemary had to admit, but as she pointed out to Vera, "It's still hearsay. Just conjecture. If everyone believed everything they heard about me, half of London would think me a murderer. If you're really worried, why don't you simply ask her?"

"I could," Vera said slowly, "or I could find out for myself. I'm betting she has more than one of those little notebooks lying around, and I'm betting they contain all the evidence we need. You know she'll deny everything if we ask, so why don't we take a peek in her dressing room and find out for ourselves."

"Oh, no," Rosemary said, holding up her free hand to wave off the suggestion. "I'm not getting involved in another one of your schemes. It's not worth the trouble," she warned.

"We can't get in trouble, Rosie. We're not children," Vera chided. "Honestly, what do you think the penalty is for breaking into someone's dressing room?" She reverted back to the southern accent then and drawled, "I think we'll be spared the guillotine." The word *guillotine* came out sounding rather odd indeed.

When Rosemary didn't immediately change her mind, Vera's nostrils flared, and she stood, arms akimbo. "Rosemary Lillywhite, I have followed you anywhere you've ever asked me to go. I've been nearly shot, almost stabbed, and practically fondled by a bunch of criminals while tottering after you! Now, I need a lookout, and by Jove, it's going to be you." By now, Vera was breathing heavily, and her face was red and pinched around the eyes.

"All right, all right," Rosemary said, standing and motioning for her friend to calm down. "You're right. I owe you one. More than one, in fact. What do you want me to do?"

"Come on," Vera said, smiling happily now that she'd got her own way. Rosemary followed her into the hallway, where she gently rapped on the door. Receiving no answer, Vera peeked into Cora's dressing room and then poked her head back out. "The coast is clear. You keep watch while I look around."

Rosemary stood in the doorway, just as Vera had requested, keeping a lookout but also taking stock of the room, and by extension, the girl to whom it belonged. Instead of a sofa, one half of Cora's dressing room held a stack of storage trunks and a large, rather wavy mirror. More mirrors hung on the walls around it in every available space, reflecting the image of whoever stood in the center back and forth across the room in a sort of kaleidoscopic illusion.

Vera marveled at the sight of herself from every imaginable angle, taking a moment to spin in a circle and observe the effect.

"Get on with it," Rosemary ordered. "We don't have

time for you to spend obsessing about how your hair looks from the back." Before opening night, Rosemary expected, Vera's dressing room would be similarly fitted out with mirrors.

When Vera spun one more time, Rosemary sniffed in annoyance and decided she'd better lend a hand.

"If we get caught in here, it will be your fault for acting the peacock. Vanity will be your downfall." There was no heat to the sentiment, but all the same, Rosemary abandoned her post at the door in favor of performing a cursory search for the notebooks. Finding positively nothing and dragging Vera out of there as fast as she possibly could was the goal.

Her hopes were dashed when, upon pulling open the bottom vanity drawer, Rosemary found something more damning than Cora's notebooks. She sucked in a breath and picked up the stack of letters written in a man's hand. To her, it was obvious that this was personal correspondence of a sensitive manner and likely had nothing whatsoever to do with Vera's fears. She moved to close the drawer again, but something caught her eye. Something that chilled Rosemary to the bone for the second time that day.

Vera heard Rosemary's sharp intake of breath and came to look over her shoulder. "Did you find them?" When she saw what Rosemary had seen, she exclaimed, "Good heavens, Rosie, is that what I think it is?"

Rosemary nodded and pulled an envelope out of the stack. Sure enough, it carried a distinctive fleur-de-lis pattern printed across the back—an exact match to the letter that had been dropped off at Rosemary's following the newspaper article detailing her connection to the Garrison Black case.

"It's only one envelope. I'd hardly call it irrefutable evidence," Rosemary hedged.

Manners dictated she refrain from peeking at Cora Flowers' personal correspondence, but if Cora *was* the one who had been hanging around her home, Rosemary needed to know. In the end, curiosity and her instinct for self-preservation won out over moral conscience.

"I told you there was something off about her!" Vera crowed. Do you think she's been using the play as an excuse to get closer to you?"

It was just like Vera to jump to conclusions. Rosemary could admit it didn't look good, but now that her heart rate had slowed and reason had returned, she felt sick to her stomach. "This isn't right, Vera. We have to get out of here."

"Nonsense, Rosie. She's odd and creepy," Vera continued. "It almost makes sense, in a twisted sort of way, for her to be the Garrison Black sympathizer."

Rosemary didn't have time to reply because from out of nowhere came a razor-edged voice. "What the hell do you think you're doing in here?" Backs to the open door, neither Rosemary nor Vera had heard anyone coming, but there was no mistaking they'd been caught in the act.

Even though it wouldn't do her any good, Rosemary dropped the letters back into the drawer and shoved it closed. "I'm terribly sorry," she said to Cora, refraining from pointing at Vera and adding, *It was all her idea!*

"You think I'm odd and creepy?" Cora asked Vera. The expression on her face was one of supreme pain, and not, it seemed, due to the snooping but more so the hurtful comments she'd overheard.

"I—I—" Vera stammered. "My apologies," she finally said, defeated. "It's just, well, you're always glaring at me and scribbling in your notebook. And then, some of the other actors said there was a problem during your last production and, you know, it seemed as though..." Vera trailed off.

Cora sighed and crossed the room, plunking her handbag down on top of one of the trunks. From its depths, she pulled a notebook, which she handed to Vera without a word.

Curiously, Vera opened the cover and began to read. Her eyebrows shot to her hairline and then furrowed as she returned her gaze to Cora. "These are notes on my performances. Very detailed and complimentary ones," she said, bewildered.

"I'm a fan," Cora said. "I was really chuffed to have been cast opposite you. Perhaps I ought to have said as much instead of feigning disinterest, but I didn't want you to think me unprofessional."

Vera tried to wrap her head around what Cora was saying, while Rosemary merely shook her head wryly. Leave it to her charismatic friend to have blown a ridiculous situation even further out of proportion.

"What about your former director?" Vera asked, having apparently decided that since she'd already been caught invading Cora's privacy, a bit more impertinence was just another drop in the bucket.

"It sounds as though you've been listening to gossip, so why don't you see for yourself," Cora huffed. She opened the drawer in which Rosemary had been snooping and pulled out the stack of letters. "I didn't know he was married. When I found out, thanks to one of the other actresses who coveted my role, I quit. It was he who refused to take no for an answer."

It only took a cursory glance to realize Cora was telling the truth. The envelopes, upon further inspection, had been sent *to* and not *from* her. Rosemary plucked the envelope with the fleur-de-lis pattern from the stack, turned it over in her hands, then put it back. Bundled with the rest, it exonerated Cora from having written the anonymous letter to Rosemary even if it was the only one like it in the pile.

Now that adrenaline wasn't coursing through her veins, she could see that perhaps it had been a stretch to believe Cora was responsible for writing the hand-delivered letter in the first place. While she pondered, Cora talked shop with Vera, explaining her very intricate process for developing a character.

"I immerse myself in *who* she is and *what* she would do in a given situation. I *become* her, and in turn, *she becomes me*." It sounded like a load of hogwash to Rosemary's ear, but Vera hung on every word. "That's why I was glaring at you. It's exactly what my character would do. That being said, our performances don't have to be a competition, nor should they."

"You didn't want the role of the sleuth after all?" Vera asked, surprised. "You're not angry because I was cast instead of you?"

Cora shook her head. "It's a great role, but I auditioned for the murderer because the character is much more complex and a complete departure from my previous work. We need the play to be a hit, and that means all of us working together as a team."

That part didn't sound so silly, Rosemary had to admit. "Cora," she interrupted suddenly, "Do you happen to know where this envelope came from?" It was a long shot, but one worth taking, so Rosemary explained why she needed to know.

"Not exactly, but my dreaded ex-director lives in the West End. Near Marylebone, so perhaps he bought it at a stationery shop on the high street there."

And that, as they say, was that, as far as Rosemary was concerned, anyway. She put the matter out of her head and listened to a few more interminable minutes of theater talk.

"I think it's brave of you to use Blackburn as your stage name. Your mother's shoes must feel impossible to fill," Cora gave what might be construed as a backhanded compliment.

Vera frowned. "Blackburn is my name, after all. What else would I use?"

Her face slightly pink now, Cora put a hand up to smooth her hair. "Of course, it is. What a silly thing for me to say." Then she brightened. "I guess that's one more thing we have in common."

When Vera frowned again, Cora continued. "Acting under our real names. Reggie doesn't, you know."

Great, Rosemary thought. *Now we've devolved into gossip. I'll never tear Vera away.*

"Do tell," Vera encouraged.

"With a surname like Hickenbottom, wouldn't you?" Cora replied with a conspiratorial grin.

Fifteen similar minutes passed before Rosemary finally managed to drag Vera away. "Come now, darling. I've missed tea, and I'm positively famished." On cue, her empty stomach ground out a growl.

"Quite so," Vera let Rosemary push her out the dressing room door. "We'll talk later, Cora, and I am sorry for snooping."

"That's quite all right. All events fall within the artist's scope, and now that I know how it feels to be hunted, I shall use the experience to enhance my character."

Her back turned to the woman, Rosemary felt no reason to school her features into a more pleasant expression.

Once settled in the car, Vera gushed, "Isn't she just the nicest girl you've ever met? And so talented, too."

If Rosemary hadn't been driving, she might have dropped her head in her hands in response to Vera's high-speed reversal concerning Cora. Instead, she changed the subject.

"What plans have you for dinner tonight? I've just dropped Desmond off to spend time with his family. I expect he'll need some cheering up after the ordeal."

Vera nodded. "He and Freddie have been cooking up some sort of scheme for that bet we made. I intended to put an end to it, but as you say, Des needs cheering, so I'll let them have their little game."

CHAPTER TWENTY-THREE

Rosemary almost forgot she'd invited Max's mother to take a tour of the back garden that afternoon. She remembered halfway through the drive home from the theater but didn't have a chance to say anything out loud as Vera dominated the conversation with talk of Cora Flowers and her intriguing acting process.

Vera, it seemed, was now convinced that to succeed, she would also need to *become her character*. And so, it was for that reason Rosemary was forced to spend an entire drive being imitated and listening to Vera's southern drawl. She contemplated taking a detour and driving straight into the river but ultimately decided that might be an extreme way to avoid paying Frederick his winnings.

She let Vera continue to wax rhapsodic and focused instead on her afternoon plans. Ariadne Whittington had been utterly delighted to have received Rosemary's request and was more than willing to offer her extensive expertise. In fact, she insisted upon coming right over to Park Road and taking a peek at the garden at Rosemary's earliest convenience.

When the plans were made, Rosemary hadn't expected to spend her morning in Whitechapel or her lunchtime breaking and entering. She sighed, knowing it would be impolite to reschedule, and more importantly, she didn't want to. Ariadne's opinion mattered greatly. Having owned a nursery, she was a fount of gardening knowledge, and she was also Max's mother. For all those reasons and more, Rosemary adored her.

That she could not drive herself galled Ariadne to no end. A self-sufficient woman, she abhorred leaning on others, even her loved ones. Yet, it couldn't be helped, and so Rosemary arranged for Wadsworth to fetch her. While he did, she made herself presentable. When bright chatter heralded Wadsworth's return, Rosemary rightly assumed Ariadne had won him over. As she greeted the woman who might, one day, become her mother-in-law, she noticed sourpuss Wadsworth wearing an uncharacteristic smile.

"Mrs. Whittington, are you quite certain you can manage the steps?" he asked, but she brushed off his concern.

"Don't make a fuss, Mr. Wadsworth," Ariadne replied, the faint note of pleasure in her voice belying her protest.

Rosemary smirked ruefully when her butler, always the gentleman, offered Ariadne his elbow. Unexpectedly, she accepted it, allowing him to guide her up the steps and through the house to the back door,

"Isn't this lovely?" Ariadne said, taking in a panoramic view of the garden from where she stood in the middle of the terrace. "I see you didn't go ripping out everything that wasn't in bloom. That's a good girl. Your landscaper knew what he was doing, certainly, but let's take a closer look."

Now that she'd made it to the lawn, there was a bit more of a spring to Ariadne's step. This was an environment where she felt completely at home, even if it was the size of a postage stamp compared to the sprawling acreage of gardens she tended with Max's father before he passed away. It comforted Rosemary to see Ariadne moving around better than she had recently. Perhaps her hip, which had given her so much trouble she'd had to move closer to her son, was finally beginning to heal.

Dash shot out the door that hadn't quite closed behind them. Barking furiously, he bounced across the lawn towards Ariadne.

"Dash, no!" Speaking sternly, Rosemary stopped him before he jumped against the older woman's legs. The last thing she Rosemary needed was for Dash to be the cause of Max's mother ending up with another injured hip.

"Hello, young fellow. Aren't you the cute one?" Ariadne bent to pet the dog, who now circled her legs, alternately sniffing and still barking. "He smells Duke."

"Probably," Rosemary bent and managed to snatch the dog on one of his circling passes. "I'll just put him back inside. He's quite friendly most of the time but can be something of a nuisance."

With the dog out from underfoot, the tour of the garden resumed. While Ariadne wandered, she pointed out and named every plant, commenting on each grouping, and gave advice that Wadsworth dutifully jotted down in a notebook he'd had tucked away in one of his pockets.

"Those damask roses are well-known for their fragrant oils. You can harvest the blossoms for herbal tea and rosewater, so you'll want to keep them pruned low enough to reach. Don't forget that masterwort needs shade to flourish. Nettle will spread out of control, as will most mint, so try to keep it separated in a corner where it can't overrun its neighbors. Oh, dear."

Ariadne stopped and pointed at the rhododendron plant Rosemary had pruned a few days prior. "Such a common mistake. Rhododendron leaves and flowers are toxic to dogs. It doesn't mean you must get rid of the plant altogether," she said when Rosemary's eyes widened with worry over little Dash. "My advice is to trim the lowest branches up out of your pup's reach. Let the creeping thyme and the ferns reclaim the space below. It will add another vertical level of plantings and give the border more dimension."

Ariadne truly was a genius, and Rosemary was grateful for her help. "We'll walk Dash on a lead until I've a chance to poison-proof the garden," she said, to which Wadsworth wholly agreed. Perhaps she'd been overly confident in her ability to manage the grounds without help. Wouldn't Wadsworth be so pleased?

"You'd be surprised how many gardens contain deadly specimens. So often, people don't bother to research what they're planting; they believe foxglove is the only beautiful poison without realizing just how many plants are, in fact, highly dangerous. Ingesting the seeds of the lovely, trumpet-shaped moonflower, for example, can induce powerful hallucinations. Deadly belladonna looks incredibly like its far less worrisome cousin, black nightshade. Even delphiniums contain high levels of aconite; every part of the flower, stem, and root, if ingested, can cause stomach problems and eventual death."

Now Rosemary knew she'd been naive to fancy herself a gardener when really, all she'd done was dig a few holes and pull a few weeds. Ariadne caught her expression and pointed out. "Don't fret, dear. I don't see anything more concerning than the rhododendron, and if you like, I'll come by periodically to ensure all is well."

Somewhere in the middle of her tour, the group of three gained another member in the form of Jack. He, too, appeared entranced by Ariadne's explanations, absorbing her every word like a sponge.

When the party had made its way closer to the area dedicated to Rosemary's crow-wooing efforts, Jack approached tentatively. "Miss Rose, I need to show you something," he said. "I think you'll be pleased. You see, they've brought you a gift."

It took a second longer than it should have for Rosemary to realize by *they*, Jack meant the crows. He pointed to one of the birdbaths, the one with the sculpture on the edge. Hanging from the marble songbird's tail feather was a gold locket—Briony Keller's, Rosemary surmised immediately. It was the only explanation; a second gold locket being found in her garden was too much of a coincidence to consider.

"Thank you, Jack," Rosemary said, pleased and relieved he'd shown such restraint. Had he wanted to, he could have nicked the chain and never told a soul. It was worth enough to tempt a dishonest person, but Rosemary wasn't surprised. The act cemented her opinion of Jack as a man with integrity. She doubted either of the other two workers would have done the same.

Vowing to offer compliments to his supervisor at a more appropriate time, Rosemary pocketed the locket, bade Jack good evening, and returned her attention to her guest.

"It's rare for crows to leave presents," Ariadne said. "They're far better at holding grudges." Her eyes watched the sky warily, and Rosemary realized Ariadne, too, could have done without the corvids she adored.

Rosemary didn't even bother to try and argue, instead merely listening to Max's mother tell a tale about a particularly vindictive murder of crows that terrorized one end of her garden for an entire year after Mr. Whittington had inadvertently disturbed a nest full of their eggs.

"The scarecrow did nothing whatsoever to help; they're not stupid. I thought I might lose my mind the way cawed at Max's father every time he left the house. It was the most hideous squawk you've ever heard. He wanted to shoot them out of the trees, but I thought that would just add fuel to their fire."

"Perhaps you've cultivated rather an optimistic view of your crow friends, Miss Rose," Wadsworth said, valiantly refraining from actually smirking.

Rosemary rejected the notion and sent him inside to fetch the tea while she and Ariadne settled at the little table on the terrace for a rest and a chat. They talked, Max's mother wanting to hear all about Vera's new play and Stella's impending birth.

"She's certain it's a girl," Rosemary gushed, "and I do

hope she's right. It would be lovely to have a reason to buy mountains of little dresses."

An odd expression crossed Ariadne's face. "Perhaps, someday, you'll have an even better reason?" Rosemary knew what the question implied, and she shifted in her seat.

"I'd hoped so, but it hasn't worked out that way," she replied noncommittally, hoping the comment would blow over.

"I'll be frank with you, dear," Ariadne admitted. "I had my reservations whether you were the right match for my son, but you managed to win me over." Internally, Rosemary snorted. Helping Ariadne solve a murder investigation that even her own chief inspector son hadn't agreed *was* a murder in the first place had gone a long way on that front.

"You're a lovely girl, Rosemary," Ariadne continued. "However, I do feel obliged to tell you: if you don't truly feel the same for Max as he feels for you, I would prefer you to be honest with him. He's a strong man, and a stoic man, but he isn't made of steel." Rosemary opened her mouth to protest but was gently shushed with a raise of Ariadne's hand.

Max arrived then, mercifully, to drive his mother home, and he wasn't alone. Constable Clayton had tagged along and appeared somewhat embarrassed or, at the very least, out of place. He smiled at Rosemary sheepishly, making her wonder if his demeanor had to do with the last time she'd seen him, from behind the counter at the Shadwell Homeless Shelter.

As if he could read her thoughts, Clayton blushed scarlet and asked, "Would it be all right if I spoke briefly with Anna?"

"Of course," Rosemary replied. "Wadsworth will escort you." She directed a pointed look towards her butler, one that indicated he was expected to keep an eye on the young maid.

Perhaps the constable had nothing at all to hide, and a perfectly acceptable explanation for his shifty behavior besides. Or maybe there was more to his story. Rosemary still thought it possible he'd been the one to turn her over to the papers, though what reason he'd have to do so she couldn't fathom. The more she mulled, the less convinced she became that financial gain would have been a compelling enough motive. It wasn't as though the papers paid a premium for tips. No, whoever talked must have done so for personal reasons.

Max interrupted her thoughts by depositing a peck on her cheek, after which he gathered his mother's things and prepared to escort her to the car.

"You're both welcome to stay for dinner," Rosemary offered. Ariadne smiled at the invitation, but Max shook his head.

"Mother needs to take her pills, don't you?" he asked,

turning her smile into a scowl. She attempted to argue, but Max stayed firm. He only appeared to regret the decision when Frederick and Vera arrived with Desmond in tow.

"Ariadne!" Frederick and Vera chorused. Desmond had yet to meet Max's mother, and so his greeting was less enthusiastic but perfectly polite, proving that he did possess manners but merely refused to use them when dealing with Max.

After allowing a few extra minutes for his mother to catch up with the new arrivals, Max again announced it was time to leave.

"Before you go, I've news," Frederick said. "Tomorrow is the big day."

When his audience failed to respond with the awe Frederick felt the announcement deserved, he rose, repeated it, then rocked backwards and forwards on his feet.

"We need more information." Rosemary frowned.

"Vera vs. Frederick in a battle to the death."

"Frederick Woolridge," Vera glared at him, "did you drink your lunch? You're making no sense whatsoever. I might want to kill you at times, but only figuratively. I have no intention of doing so otherwise."

Desmond snorted out a laugh.

"A figure of speech, my love," Frederick rushed to put Vera's mind at ease. "I'm talking about a rematch of the

Easter Egg incident." He buffed his nails on his lapel. "Des cooked it up. He's setting out an obstacle course in the park. Winner takes all."

"I'd like to revise my earlier statement. To the death sounds fine with me." Vera managed to look annoyed and amused at the same time.

Rosemary explained she and Vera were, for the morning anyway, indisposed with LLV business, and the group decided, after a short discussion, that the competition would commence at half-past-one the next afternoon.

After Max had gone and the others as well, Rosemary's mind refused to settle. Her thoughts kept returning to young Clayton with chilling results. She ought to have been used to the sensation but discovered she was not. *Whoever had talked to the papers must have done so for personal reasons.* The notion replayed through her mind. Max's constable was young—not more than twenty-one if she recalled correctly.

Was it conceivable? Could sweet, bumbling Constable Clayton be the spawn of mass murderer Garrison Black?

Chapter Twenty-Four

Vera wasn't nearly as open-minded or optimistic as Rosemary had been when she caught her first glimpse of the Shadwell Homeless Shelter and its surroundings. She raised a dubious eyebrow and cast a doubtful look in her friend's direction, muttering something about the 'vigilantes' under her breath, but once inside, set to work at a pace rivaling that of even the most seasoned volunteer.

"She's really taking to the work," Esme said to Rosemary, nodding across the room to where Vera swapped out dirty cot linens for clean. Where cots were occupied, she offered a smile, gentle words, and a soothing touch.

"She's taking to the people," Rosemary corrected with a misty smile. "She'll have them all back up on their feet in no time, following her around adoringly."

Esme nodded and replied, "Whatever it takes. It's a worthy cause. I hope the ladies don't tire of lending a hand. This place can use all the help it can get."

Rosemary followed Esme's gaze to where Hadley worked a mop over a section of the dining hall floor. "I don't quite think this is what she had in mind when she suggested we volunteer."

"No, certainly not," Esme made a sound that Rosemary would have called a snort if it hadn't been so dainty. "Though what she did expect, I couldn't say. Perhaps she thinks all these men need is a good spit and polish."

"If only it were as simple as all that," Rosemary agreed, thinking the entire building needed an actual spit and polish, and then she and Esme each returned to their respective tasks. For Rosemary, that meant scrubbing what seemed like years of dirt from the floor-to-ceiling windows lining the entrance hall.

An hour and a quarter later, with the help of a stepladder she'd dug out of the broom cupboard, Rosemary had managed to significantly improve the state of two windows out of ten and felt as though she'd attended one of Ivy's advanced calisthenics sessions. She had also managed to break two of her fingernails and then made herself bleed when she'd raked one of the jagged edges across her cheek.

Vera always kept a full manicure set in her handbag, and so Rosemary ducked down a short hallway adjacent to the entrance hall and into the small office where

Penny had assured their personal belongings would be safe.

Inside, on a desk that was obviously seldom-used, sat fifteen handbags in various shapes and colors. Rosemary tried to remember which one had been Vera's, but unfortunately, her friend owned countless bags, and there was no telling which one was hers. She peeked back out of the office in search of Vera but realized she must either be in the kitchen or one of the common rooms.

Instead of hunting her down, Rosemary went back inside and found her own purse. She found her handkerchief, which she used to wipe the now-drying blood off her cheek, and then searched the rest of the purse for a nail file knowing the attempt was futile.

It made sense that the handbag sitting next to hers ought to have been Vera's, and the blue satin lining looked familiar enough Rosemary was almost certain it belonged to her friend. She opened it, rummaged around inside, and did indeed come up with a nail file.

Quickly, she did what she needed to do and returned the file to the bag. As she did, Rosemary noticed a stack of letters inside. It seemed everywhere she looked lately, there was a stack of letters! Except who would Vera be writing? Rosemary knew her friend to be a terrible pen-pal. She'd send the occasional postcard, but correspondence was not one of Vera's strong suits.

Curious, Rosemary took a peek, knowing her friend wouldn't mind, and if she did, Rosemary would accept the consequences. Her face reddened when she noted the name on the envelopes and realized it wasn't Vera's handbag she'd been rooting through but Hadley Walsh's. All of the letters had been sent to a Marylebone address Rosemary recognized as not terribly far from her own house.

Ashamed of herself now, she moved to tuck the stack back into the handbag when the return address caught her eye: *HM Prison Pentonville*, above which was scrawled not a name but a number—a prisoner number, Rosemary surmised. From the looks of it, Hadley was on close enough terms with one of the inmates to warrant regular correspondence.

Rosemary flipped to the next letter in the stack and noted with surprise that the return address read *HM Prison Brixton* on this envelope. Another had been sent to Wandsworth, each with different prisoner numbers written in a different hand.

She couldn't stop herself, and in that moment, Rosemary didn't care if Max's accusation had been justified. Her fingers shook as she opened the first letter, and after a few lines, they began to tremble for an entirely different reason. Rosemary felt the heat rise to her face, and she felt certain if she wanted to, she could spit nails.

Hadley Walsh was something else. Rosemary didn't even know what word to use. Inmate lover? Criminal sympathizer? Deranged lunatic? She ripped open the next one and read further, hardly able to believe her eyes.

"What do you think you're doing?" Hadley screeched from the doorway where she and half of the group, including Esme, Ivy, and Vera, stood poised to enter. For the second time in two days, she found herself caught, her hands a bright crimson color that screamed of her guilt.

Incensed, Rosemary shot back, "What do you think *you're* doing, Hadley? What kind of person actually wants to associate with convicted murderers?"

All eyes turned to Hadley now, and had she not been so disgusted with the contents of the letters, she might have felt bad for exposing her secret in front of the entire LLV.

"Give me back my property, you nosy old snoop!" Hadley seethed, never taking her eyes off Rosemary and no longer caring what anyone else in the group overheard.

Unfortunately for Hadley, she hadn't known that speaking to Rosemary like that in front of Vera was one of the worst choices she could have made. Before she knew it, Vera had Hadley by the arm in an attempt to hold her back from lunging at her friend.

What *Vera* hadn't known was that Hadley, as tiny and inconsequential as she may have looked, proved herself a natural at the LLV's self-defense instructions, and knew exactly how to use Vera's weight and momentum against her.

Hadley shifted, used her hip as a fulcrum, and Vera's arm as a lever of sorts. Shock painted Vera's face as her feet left the floor. From the flat of her back, she blinked up at Hadley, surprise turning to fury.

Rosemary had a trick of her own up her sleeve, and instead of waiting for Hadley to catapult across the office and rip the letters from her hand, she circled around to the back of the desk and shoved the handbags off the top in one fell swoop. Cosmetic compacts bounced, and key rings jingled. Coin purses tumbled to the floor, taking Hadley back and buying Rosemary a few precious moments.

There was something she suspected but needed to confirm. She reached back into the handbag and fished around until she found what she was looking for: a piece of stationery with the remainder of a shopping list printed on it in small, cramped letters, and across the top, a fleur-de-lis pattern to seal Hadley's fate.

"It was you!" Now it was Rosemary's turn to seethe. "You wrote that horrible note and dropped it off at my home."

Vera appeared torn between rushing to Rosemary's

rescue or staying out of the fray to avoid getting pummeled. Again.

"You deserved it!" Hadley retorted. "You think you're above the law because you're dating a chief inspector, but you're nothing more than a common criminal, and your time is running out. Any day now, an honest detective will figure out how to prove what you've done, and you'll get the comeuppance you deserve for murdering Garrison Black!"

"I've done no such thing." Rosemary's face flamed with the heat of her denial. "But I'll tell you this much, if he'd have managed to get into my house as planned, and I'd have had the chance, I would have killed him without hesitation."

"Do you see?" Hadley appealed to the LLV for support. "She has murder in her heart."

"I'd feel the same as Rosemary if Black came after me," Maddy spoke up. She ignored the second half of Hadley's accusation. "I bet we all would." Voices rose in assent while Hadley fumed. "You're twisted if you don't, and I'm glad Rosemary filched those letters, or we would never have known how sadly lacking you are in character."

"Hear, hear." Minerva patted Maddy on the shoulder hard enough to make Maddy flinch.

Ivy stepped forward and held up a hand to command silence. "I vote we oust Hadley from the group."

Every hand save Rosemary's and Hadley's shot into the air.

"What about Rosemary?" Hadley demanded. "Will you willingly have a sneak thief in your group?"

"I didn't realize it was her bag until I'd seen the letters, but I will, of course, abide by any decision you make with regards to my membership," Rosemary bent her head and waited for Ivy to call for a vote. Reluctantly, Ivy did. No one was surprised when Hadley's was the only hand to take the air.

"Your vote no longer counts," Ivy told her with no small sense of satisfaction, but the fracas effectively ruined the mood of the day. Members dispersed in groups of two and three, leaving Rosemary and Vera the last ones to leave.

Upon approaching the counter in the entrance hall to bid the sour-faced Penny a pleasant day, Rosemary overheard a snippet of a conversation between two of the paid staff.

"He's disappeared again," the first one said, her voice filled with concern.

The other replied flippantly, "Probably off on another bender."

Penny shooed them back to work with a comment of her own, "Don't judge poor Mr. Clayton so harshly. He's got his demons just like they all do. He'll come back eventually. You'll see. He always does."

Stunned, Rosemary opened her mouth to ask Penny if Mr. Clayton was related to the constable, Morris Clayton, but she never had the chance because, across the entrance hall, she caught sight of her late brother's doppelganger. Her options were limited; stay and find out more about Mr. Clayton or get Vera out of there before *she* saw the man and experienced a visceral reaction.

One look at Vera's face reduced the options to none. Besides, Penny wasn't the question-answering type, and Rosemary found one coincidence per day—Cora's ex-director and Hadley shopping in the same stationers—more than enough. The Clayton men *not* being related would make two, and that was one too many.

It was a question for another time, but for now, Rosemary grabbed Vera's arm and pulled her, forcefully, towards the door. "We've got to go," she said, "or we'll be late for Freddie's comeuppance."

Chapter Twenty-Five

Rosemary was still reeling from the confrontation with Hadley when she arrived back at the townhouse to prepare for the big obstacle course showdown. Desmond had enlisted the help of Wadsworth and Anna, with Gladys citing urgent housekeeping tasks as an excuse to decline the invitation.

When after Vera hurried upstairs to change her clothes and pin up her hair, Rosemary found the cook, quite free indeed, out on the terrace sipping a cup of tea and enjoying the view, she couldn't help but chuckle.

"They're all over in the park," Gladys explained with positively no remorse, gesturing towards the gate, "and they took Dash with them. The inspector phoned, as well, to say he might be late and to go ahead and start without him."

"Frederick will retell the whole event several times over before the day's end, anyhow," Rosemary replied. "Max will feel as though he experienced every moment in vivid detail." Gladys's eyes twinkled, but she diplomatically refrained from agreeing with Rosemary's estimation.

Vera bounded down the stairs looking as though she was headed into battle.

"I've borrowed your sparring outfit," she said. "The fit on the trousers is a bit loose, but I can move." To prove the point, Vera ran through a series of squats and lunges before jogging in place

She pulled Rosemary through the gate and across the grass, and then stood in front of Frederick, arms akimbo. "Let's not dally," she said, nodding at Desmond to begin the proceedings and pointing skyward, "or we'll be caught out in the rain."

Wadsworth took the opportunity to beg off, ambling back across the grass with Dash nipping at his heels. Anna, however, had no intention of going anywhere. "This is better than a church fête," she said.

"Ladies and gentleman," Desmond announced in a fair imitation of a circus ringmaster, "it's Frederick Woolridge versus Vera Woolridge in today's competition! The winner goes home with—" he paused for dramatic effect, "absolutely nothing!" He received a glare from Vera that only widened his smile.

Frederick boomed, "That's not true, Des old boy—the winner gets to lord his win over the loser for the rest of her life!"

"You're not half as funny as you think you are, husband," Vera retorted and then turned to Rosemary with fire in her eyes. "I am going to show you what a dame can do when she puts her mind to it."

"All right, then," Rosemary laughed. She sincerely hoped Vera succeeded in taking Frederick down a notch. It would serve him right for all the times he behaved like an insufferable braggart after winning a contest or a bet.

Quite proud of himself for conceiving the idea all on his own, Desmond explained the rules. "First up is the bucket toss. You'll stand back here," he pointed towards the ground, at two X marks made out of crossed tree branches, "and throw until you make three baskets." Desmond indicated a pair of buckets positioned some fair distance away. He handed them each three lengths of plaited rope tied into a knot on each end, just like the ones Dash loved to fetch.

"When you've finished, don't forget to grab your flag and hold on tightly," Desmond warned and then explained the rest of the challenges. "Whoever reaches the top of the church tower having collected a flag from each of the obstacles, and retrieves the final red flag first, will be declared the winner. Rosemary, I'll need you at the top of the tower as judge. You can see everything from up there, so you'll also need to make sure these two stay honest. Does everyone understand the rules?" he asked, glancing between the two contestants.

Frederick nodded once, his eyes scanning the park and the obstacles with determination. Vera gave a clipped, "Understood," and lowered into a lunge position to stretch out her calves.

Rosemary accepted her assignment and hurried off towards the porticoed entrance to the church tower. Four flights of enclosed stairs led to the open belfry where she could watch the competition with a birds-eye view. By the time she reached the top, she was out of breath with both exertion and excitement. Once she was in position, Rosemary leaned out over the waist-high railing and waved to Desmond.

He hollered loud enough for Rosemary to hear, "On your marks, get set, and GO!"

The combatants took off, Frederick beating Vera to the X mark by a few seconds. His first two tosses went entirely wild, landing closer to Vera's bucket than his own. From her time spent playing fetch with Dash, Rosemary knew that the two knotted ends skewed the weight distribution, making the rope fly in odd directions. It had taken her some time to work out how best to adjust her aim.

With Vera trailing only slightly behind, Frederick hit his mark first and grabbed his flag with an exuberant "whoop!" She, in turn, outpaced him on the next obstacle, a series of balance beams Desmond had constructed using some of the wood scraps from the old potting shed.

They were neck-and-neck, then, but the pace was poised to slow with the next task: a challenging tree climb that Rosemary, for one, felt might have been going a bit too far. During Desmond's unveiling, she'd voiced the concern, but neither Frederick nor Vera had been put off enough to eliminate the competition's piece de resistance.

While the pair began to climb, Rosemary took in the view of her back garden below. She could see that Gladys had taken Dash inside, leaving the terrace deserted. From her elevated vantage point, the garden resembled a map of the countryside, the walkways representing roads, curling snake-like around clusters of planting bed villages. It was an image Rosemary felt certain she could turn into a beautiful painting.

Her artistic pursuits would have to wait, however, because the competition was now fully underway. Frederick had made it partway up his tree before realizing that he'd miscalculated, taken the wrong route, and now had to backtrack. Vera had gotten off to a slower start but chose the correct path and was now picking up the pace to try and gain the lead.

From somewhere in the distance, the shrill caw of a crow rent the air. At once, two thoughts struck Rosemary. The first was that the caw sounded like the same one her feathered friends made every time Jack entered the garden—one of dislike, or at least, one of warning. The second was that she—or really, Desmond—had invaded the space where the birds kept their nest, and it was that notion that left her feeling unsettled.

She knew her friends all believed her somewhat deranged for having come to fancy the crows in the first place, but the truth was she quite enjoyed their playful nature and had learned to respect their intelligence and indeed wonder, at times, if they were smarter than some of the humans she'd met.

The last thing she wanted was to shoo them from their nest or give them cause to turn against her. As Ariadne had pointed out, the birds were quite capable of holding grudges, and Rosemary had no desire to be on the receiving end of their ire.

That being said, with Frederick and Vera both still shimmying up the branches of their respective trees, Rosemary had been left with a few moments to spare and found herself intrigued by the nest tucked beneath one of the eaves. She inched closer, vowing to only take a peek, when something caught her eye.

A piece of stationery fluttered in the breeze, white streaked with black, faded but familiar enough that Rosemary's blood ran cold. It was the third time in as many days that the sight of a sheet of paper had elicited a similar reaction, but this time was different. This wasn't some hastily-penned recrimination or a vaguely threatening note; it was a Garrison Black original charcoal drawing, and in it, his subject—Rosemary—was quite undoubtedly dead. Over the spot where her heart would be, he had scribbled a version of his calling card—the shriveled black heart that had haunted Rosemary's dreams.

It wasn't a leap to conclude that the crows, as unapologetic scavengers, might have nicked the drawing from Black's overcoat pocket the night he died. Still, finding it there, that way was unsettling and suddenly, Rosemary wished the competition would end. Black *had* been in her garden that night with the intent of murdering her in her own home! She had spent so much time insisting she wasn't frightened of what he intended to do to her, she almost believed the words herself. Now that she was out of danger, Rosemary could see how naive she'd been and how frustrating her stubbornness must have been for her friends.

She returned to the railing, took a few deep breaths to calm herself, and searched the trees for her brother and Vera. Surely, they both ought to have snagged their flags by now. Sure enough, Frederick had descended to the ground and was running towards the final obstacle, but before he could make it halfway across the grass, his wife let out a scream that stopped him in his tracks.

"Ahhh!" Vera yelled as a branch broke under her foot and she began to fall.

Rosemary turned, all thoughts of the crows and Garrison Black having flown. All she could think about was getting to her dearest friend. All she could hear was the sound of Vera's frightened scream echoing through her head even after it had ceased. So focused was Rosemary she nearly bowled over a figure standing at the bottom of the second-level landing.

"Miss Keller!" she said, surprised. "What are you doing here?" Rosemary looked around the woman and pressed forward, but Briony side-stepped to stay in front of her.

"I've come for my locket, of course," she said. If Rosemary didn't hear the acid in her tone, who could blame her? Vera's safety was of the utmost concern. "I'd like it back, please."

Rosemary opened her mouth to tell Briony she could find the locket waiting for her at the house but stopped short. Wouldn't Wadsworth have returned the necklace had Briony rung the doorbell? With a start, Rosemary realized that it would have been impossible for him to do so since the locket was still in her cardigan pocket.

As she reached in to retrieve it, the Garrison Black charcoal drawing fell to the floor between herself and Briony. Rosemary's eyes flicked between it and the woman's face, which was now white as a sheet and arranged in an unfathomable expression.

She drew herself up and dropped the act. Her fingers tightened around the cane she clutched in her right hand. Her jaw hardened, and in an instant, Briony went from a lame, near-elderly lady to a cougar, poised to pounce.

"Locket. Now!"

Her mind racing, Rosemary tried to figure out why her instincts told her she was in danger. It happened more frequently than she cared to admit, but usually, she knew *why* because usually, it meant she had just solved a murder investigation.

The irony took a moment to dawn on Rosemary—a precious moment she didn't really have to spare. The whole case flipped over and settled into new lines.

For once, the papers had been right. Garrison Black hadn't died of natural causes on her doorstep; he'd been murdered. She wasn't certain how or why, but she was convinced Briony Keller was responsible. The crows had stolen the drawings off Black's body, and they'd also stolen Briony's lost locket. Certainly, they could have done so on separate occasions, but if Rosemary knew one thing about a murder case, it was that true coincidences were both few and far between.

Instinctively, she pulled the locket from her cardigan and opened it with shaking fingers. Inside, the face of a newborn baby, the photograph so faded it was barely visible, looked out from the heart-shaped frame.

Eyes falling on the image, Briony took in a sharp breath, her hand reached out involuntarily as if to satisfy a deeply-felt longing. The final piece of the puzzle fell into place for Rosemary.

"You—you were Garrison Black's lover!" Rosemary exclaimed, her words punctuated by an ominous crash of thunder in the distance.

Chapter Twenty-Six

Briony's eyes lit upon the glint of the gold locket and then turned black as coal. She tightened her grip on the cane and let out a strangled cry that raised the hair on the back of Rosemary's neck.

Rosemary's heart stopped, then lurched in her chest before thumping wildly. Vividly, a vision from the alley the night of the Kettner's dinner flashed before her eyes. The knife-wielding attacker had worn the same expression Briony did now, and Rosemary felt certain she was in danger.

She also felt fairly certain she could take Briony in a bare-knuckle fight, and perhaps she might even be able to disarm the older woman. However, if Rosemary had learned one thing from the LLV's self-defense classes, it was that one ought never to underestimate one's opponent, and Briony's cane evened the odds a bit.

As Rosemary saw it, she had two choices, take her chances with the cane and try to get past Briony, or lure the older woman to the one place Rosemary might be able to summon help. The knob on the cane looked solid enough to cave someone's head in, so the latter seemed the obvious choice.

"He wasn't capable of anything other than hate," Briony seethed, bringing Rosemary back to the present and the problem at hand, "so the label of *lover* is wholly incorrect. That man ruined my life." She inched closer, her eyes brimming with unshed tears. Rosemary matched her step for step, backing slowly up the stairs.

Her instincts screamed that the murder was one of retribution, and Briony's statement only served as confirmation. In Rosemary's mind, a nebulous plan began to form. She thought about old Mrs. Brighton's story and, even though it took a great effort, managed to maintain a sympathetic tone when she asked, "You gave birth to his child, didn't you? It must have been awful for you, truly. I couldn't possibly imagine."

At the mention of the baby, Briony softened infinitesimally, but then her expression turned wild, and she snapped, "How did you know? And who did you tell?" She looked as though she'd love nothing more than to tear Rosemary limb from limb.

"I didn't tell anyone," Rosemary insisted, channeling Vera's acting skills and infusing her voice with as much reassurance as she could muster. "The only other person who knows is Mrs. Brighton, Black's old landlady."

Briony's eyes flashed at the words *other person who knows*. Rosemary realized she had miscalculated and made an attempt to control the damage. If by some chance, Briony landed enough blows with the cane to walk away from this encounter, Mrs. Brighton would be in danger.

"Mrs. Brighton is a sweet, elderly lady," she lied. *Sour* would have been a far more appropriate adjective, but Rosemary didn't need Briony to know that. "She never told a soul all these years, but she suspected you were in trouble and knew you were an innocent. All this time, she kept your secret so you and the baby might live a normal life."

The words, meant to convey that Mrs. Brighton—and Rosemary by extension—was an ally rather than an enemy, had a mildly soothing effect on Briony that still did absolutely nothing to calm Rosemary's fear.

"I could never live a normal life after what he did to me." Briony cried, her voice verging on a whine. "He was always a monster. I just didn't see the signs. Not until it was too late." The words sounded like an oft-repeated mantra of self-pity, which did nothing to garner more sympathy—in fact, Briony's attitude had the opposite effect on Rosemary.

"You were so young; how could you have known?" she said in a tone she might use with her little nephew, Nelly, if he were having a temper tantrum. "Garrison

Black was a sick and twisted man. He beat you, didn't he?"

Briony hadn't said as much, but Rosemary put the pieces together even as she realized that Mrs. Brighton had left some details out of her description of the evening Briony fled Black's flat. "It's all right," she soothed. "He tried to hurt me, too, but we're safe now. You did the right thing. He deserved to die."

Briony nodded and repeated the phrase. "He deserved to die. I did the right thing."

Rosemary took the opportunity to further her escape plan, taking a step back and luring Briony to follow. "Tell me about it," she said softly, hoping against hope that she had laid sufficient groundwork and could tempt Briony into talking long enough to get her to the belfry. In Rosemary's experience, crazed murderers loved to explain just exactly how and why they'd done what they'd done.

For a long moment, Briony contemplated whether to answer, and then, eyes still on her locket, she began to speak. "There's not much to tell. I worked as a waitress in my uncle's diner when he started coming around and trying to woo me. He could be charming when it suited him. Had I any sense, I never would have taken up with the likes of him, but he had me convinced he was in love. Convinced enough to do things I knew I shouldn't—to defile myself in the eyes of God."

While she talked, Rosemary noticed Briony refused to speak Black's name, and every time Rosemary did, Briony winced, and her eyes grew a little wilder.

"That night—that awful, final night—he let me in the flat, went out to buy fags, and when he came back, he saw a man exiting the building. He went into a rage, accusing me of having entertained the man—I'd done nothing of the sort, of course, but he wouldn't listen."

Rosemary had been right. For so long, Briony had kept her secrets to herself, and now she was bursting with the need for her story to be heard. Rosemary counted the fact a blessing, keeping her features schooled into a sympathetic expression while Briony talked.

"He said that since I'd been willing to engage in a physical relationship with *him* without being married, it stood to reason I couldn't be trusted not to do the same with any other man." Her eyebrows drew together then, and she cursed. "As if it had been my doing alone. I'd been prepared to tell him about the baby, but I never had the chance. He wouldn't listen to me, couldn't see reason. He called me his angel, but still, he hit me. Over and over—I don't know how many times—then he left me there. I think he thought I was far worse off, but I managed to collect myself and get away."

Rosemary could hear the rain, louder now, as she led Briony higher up into the tower. "You ran?" she prompted.

"I ran," Briony confirmed. "I got on a train and rode it as far as I could, to the other side of England, to a little village in the countryside. Yet, I couldn't bear to keep the baby. I wanted a better life for him, and I knew, somehow, that if his existence was ever discovered, he would never be safe. So, I gave him up. For a long time, I wondered if I should have kept him after all, but then, when the murders began, and the papers described the calling card with the black heart—I knew."

"The black heart?"

Briony nodded and pulled her gaze from the locket to link eyes with Rosemary. "When the mood was on him, he used to say there were women who looked like angels but were nothing more than devils poised to steal the heart of a man and turn it black. That's how I knew it was him; there was no mistake. I had made the right choice."

Sergeant Prescott had wondered about the significance of Black's calling card for years. It was one more piece of the puzzle solved, but it would matter little if Rosemary wasn't alive to tell the tale.

"I was the only one who could identify him, and I knew if I kept quiet, he would continue to cut a swath through London. Yet, I still couldn't bring myself to go to the police."

"You were the one who called in the anonymous tip!"

Rosemary exclaimed, but Briony scoffed.

"What good did it do? The police still couldn't catch him! It took them years to get him into a cell. By then, I'd returned to the city. My uncle had passed away, and my aunt needed help. I thought I had been away long enough that I would be safe. Then, lo and behold, he broke out, and eventually, he walked back into the diner. When he did, he looked right through me—didn't even know who I was! Well, I recognized him, of course, and that's when I started to formulate a plan. All those years in the countryside, I'd learned a thing or two about plants. A few chunks of aconite root added to his stew, and he wouldn't be long for this world."

Rosemary recalled Ariadne's tour of the garden and her description of several deadly poisons commonly mistaken for garden flowers. When she discovered Black's body, his coat had smelled faintly of vomit. At the time, she hadn't thought much of it because the coroner cited natural causes, but now Rosemary realized it had been a clue. She had been so content to believe he had simply died at an opportune moment, she ignored the signs of foul play.

Pivoting around the corner enough to look up, Rosemary's heart sinking when she realized they weren't yet at the top of the tower; another landing preceded one more flight of stairs. She could hear the pitter-patter of rain as it began to fall on the roof above and knew she had to keep Briony calm and talking if she was going to make it to the top with hopes of flagging down Desmond and her brother.

"Why not simply go to the police then?"

Briony scoffed and spat, "They were barely able to catch him the first time, even with my help, and then still he managed to escape. That night, I watched him, scribbling away in his notebook, and realized he'd set his sights on a new victim: you. Of course, I didn't know who you were, but I knew if I acted quickly, I could save your life. I knew it was up to me to stop him. At least this way, I could be certain he wouldn't ever harm anyone else."

Though her reasons were misguided, Briony truly believed she'd done the right thing. A small part of Rosemary agreed. Still, Briony's justification for murder didn't change the fact she was mad as a hatter. While she hadn't issued an outright threat, Rosemary couldn't tell exactly what her intentions were.

"Now your son not only has a murderer for a father— he has one for a mother, as well." The comment popped out of Rosemary's mouth before she'd had time to think it through. A second too late, it occurred to her that antagonizing the woman probably wasn't her best-laid plan.

"Better him than you, wouldn't you say?" Briony retorted hotly. "Would you have preferred I let him kill you?" The question was rhetorical, or at least Rosemary was content to let it go unanswered, and it didn't matter anyway because now it seemed Briony couldn't have stopped herself if she wanted to. She continued to tell her story while Rosemary backed up the last two stairs.

"I followed him from the diner to your house."

Rosemary held the locket in her outstretched hand, swinging it gently back and forth, almost like a hypnotist's pendulum. She felt her window of opportunity begin to close and picked up her pace.

"He'd slowed, by then, of course," Briony said, following Rosemary and the locket. "I could hardly believe he'd made it that far. In the dark, and considering the discomfort he must have been in, he didn't notice me following him. He hadn't realized I'd ducked in through the gate behind him. I could see you in your bedroom window. You looked like an innocent, someone who didn't deserve what he had in store for you."

A shudder ran through Rosemary when Briony drove home the fact that, without intervention, she might have died that night.

"He watched you, too, and called you his angel. I couldn't take it anymore, so I stepped into the light from your window and told him he wouldn't know an angel if one jumped out and bit him."

Good for her, Rosemary thought, then realized how

stupid it was to root for a murderer.

"He knew me then and would have done for me if he could, but it was too late. He swayed, began to fall, and I knew it was time, so I lunged and shoved him as hard as I could. He fell into the wheelbarrow resting near your terrace. It wasn't until later I realized I'd lost my necklace in the process. Once again, that man was to be my downfall."

Rosemary had been correct; the crime was one of retribution, of opportunity, and yet somehow also premeditated. Unless she was very much mistaken, Briony carried no shred of regret.

Now, they'd reached the belfry, and Rosemary could see her brother and Desmond down below, tending to Vera's ankle, their focus quite clearly directed away from the church tower. Then, like a knight in shining armor, she saw Max coming across the grass with Clayton by his side.

Her face must have betrayed her relief because Briony's gaze shifted to take in the scene below. She recognized Max, and suddenly, any camaraderie the pair had shared dissolved in the falling rain. Perhaps, Rosemary thought wildly, if she had truly *become* her sympathetic character, her acting might have been more convincing.

As it stood, The jig was up.

"This is how you repay my kindness?" Briony

demanded. "I did the city of London a service, and now you're content to send me to the gallows?" She raised the cane, drew herself up to her full height, and suddenly appeared quite formidable, indeed.

"If you come clean," Rosemary said, her eyes flicking to where Max still had yet to notice her predicament, "they'll go easy on you. It was self-defense." Rosemary thought she was more likely to make headway with a diminished capacity plea, considering Briony was far from in her right mind, but wisely she kept that notion to herself.

"I should have let him kill you!" Briony seethed.

Rosemary opened her mouth and shouted all of Frederick's codewords that came to mind, "Googly-ho-spiffing-tally-biffer!" They came out sounding like one long word.

Caught off-guard, Briony lunged, but Rosemary deftly sidestepped the attack, allowing Briony to take hold of the locket rather than *her*. She didn't expect for the force of the momentum to launch Briony over the top of the belfry's railing.

Rosemary gasped and scrambled after her, leaning over the ledge, unexpectedly relieved to discover that Briony hadn't plummeted to her death. Instead, she clung to the railing, but Rosemary could see she was quickly losing her grip.

Several feet below, the portico roof might break

Briony's fall, or it might seal her fate. It was a risk, to be certain, and one Rosemary didn't think would come out in Briony's favor.

By now, her friends realized what was happening, and all four of the men were running across the grass towards the church tower. She could tell they weren't going to arrive in time to make the save.

Rosemary looked into Briony's eyes, saw the fear etched in them, and knew she had a choice to make. She could either let Briony fall, or she could take action. Ultimately, Rosemary decided she was neither judge nor jury, nor did she have any desire to be either. Whatever Briony deserved, it wasn't her choice to deliver the sentence.

"Please," Briony pleaded.

Compelled, Rosemary hiked one leg over the rail, found a foothold, and reached down to grasp Briony's arms. Up, up, she pulled with all her might until Briony's hands found purchase around Rosemary's biceps.

All she had to do now was pull the woman back up to safety. It should have been easy, but before Rosemary could catch her breath, the clock struck the hour, and the church bell began to peal. While the sound was lilting and pleasant from a distance, there in the church tower, the bell vibrated with enough force to cause Rosemary to startle and lose her grip.

Frederick and Desmond had scaled the portico then and were poised for the catch, but Briony's gaze was locked on Rosemary, and she couldn't see them. "Let go," Rosemary urged, which only caused Briony to cling tighter.

If Briony took Rosemary down with her, their combined weight would overpower the men. A quick vision passed through Rosemary's head where locked together, she and Briony cannonballed into the two men, and all four of them ended as smashed bodies on the ground.

Digging deep, Rosemary jammed her knee harder against the rail, yanked with all her might. Her shoulder exploded with pain, but the small movement allowed Briony to look down and see her saviors.

"Let go," Rosemary ordered again. This time, Briony did.

***

The young constable, Morris Clayton, reached the belfry first, a few strides ahead of Max and far less out of breath. Anna arrived next, her face wet with tears, and rushed to her mistress's side.

"I'm all right," Rosemary said, wincing, "but I'm going to need a doctor." Her shoulder hung at an odd angle, and despite her calm demeanor, it hurt worse than anything Rosemary had ever experienced.

"My father was a medic in the war," Clayton said calmly, out of nowhere. "I can help if you'll let me. I know how to pop your shoulder back into the socket. It won't be pleasant, but when it's in place, it will feel like a relief—at least, until the tenderness sets in."

Max's eyes widened, but Rosemary looked into Clayton's eyes and, even through the pain, knew he was certain. At any rate, she didn't think she could bear waiting for an ambulance, and so she nodded in assent despite Max's obvious reservations.

"Trust me," she said, and for once, Max did.

Constable Clayton looked at his supervisor. "I'm going to need your help, sir. Get her on her feet and hold her steady, just like that," he explained how Max was to position himself and then came around to Rosemary's injured side. "I want you to take a deep breath and, on my count of three, let it out."

Rosemary did as she was told, impressed with the way the young constable gripped her shoulder with confidence and shoved it, forcefully, back into place. She did experience an immense feeling of relief for a moment, and then the pain returned, albeit at a much lower level than before.

"Thank you, constable," Rosemary said, thinly but sincerely, as she rotated her shoulder and attempted a smile. She could have grinned like a child on Christmas morning and still not have matched the look of adoration painted across Anna's face. The girl was even more smitten now than she had been before, not that Rosemary could blame her.

She found herself sinking into Max's arms and felt as though she could stay there for a very long time. It was not to be so.

"I have to—," Max reluctantly pulled away.

"I understand. Go. Do your job. Be a policeman."

Chapter Twenty-Seven

"Miss Rose, your mother is on the line," Anna poked her head into Rosemary's bedroom, where she and Vera sat propped up in bed, side-by-side. With Rosemary's arm in a sling and Vera's ankle elevated on a pile of cushions, they made rather a pathetic sight. "She sounds excited."

Frederick hadn't even grumbled, at least not out loud, or where he could be overheard, about being relegated to the guest room. He could have gone home, but it felt far too empty without Vera, and even though he knew the danger was truly over, he preferred to stay close by his wife and sister.

It had been three days since the event that was now referred to as *the incident* in hushed tones, and Rosemary had to admit she didn't hate being waited on hand and foot. She left Vera quite contentedly picking through a box of chocolates and hurried downstairs to the telephone. "How is she?" Rosemary asked immediately, skipping over the customary polite greeting.

For once, Evelyn didn't scold. Instead, she replied excitedly, "Your sister is just fine—exhausted but in high spirits, and we've got a beautiful baby girl!" Stella had been right; the baby *had* been a girl. Tears sprang to Rosemary's eyes, unbidden but not unexpected. "Wait until you hear what they named her," Evelyn preened. "Evelyn Rose. Can you believe it? Stella says they'll call her Lyn for short. Isn't that grand?"

Now, the tears streamed down Rosemary's face. It was quite grand, but that didn't mean she ought to fall to pieces. "I'm properly amazed," Rosemary said aloud, wiping her eyes on a handkerchief pulled from the telephone desk, "and I can't wait to meet my new niece."

"The best part is, she's dispensed with her insane idea to sail off to America. Honestly, did we learn nothing from the *Titanic*, the *Empress of Ireland*, or the *Lusitania*? Every one of my friends who have traveled across the Atlantic says not to believe a thing you read in the brochures. The accommodations on those steamships are positively horrendous! And what do you suppose people do when they get there and can't find a proper cup of tea? It's simply not worth the trouble."

Evelyn took a while longer than usual to wind down, and even though Rosemary smiled ruefully during her diatribe, for once, she wasn't searching for an excuse to beg off the call. "For now, at least, it's a moot point, Mother," she simply said. "Rejoice in the fact she's staying around and not taking the children away for several months."

That set her mother off on another tangent, followed by a thorough third degree during which Rosemary was required to assure her she and Vera were both just fine. At least Evelyn's attention would be focused on Stella for the foreseeable future. Perhaps she might even let Vera alone.

The thought brought a smile to Rosemary's face, and she shook her head. A sprained ankle might buy Vera a couple of weeks, but wild horses couldn't drag Evelyn away from her mission to ensure the Woolridge name lived on through Frederick.

By the time she returned to her bedroom, Vera had fallen asleep, so Rosemary shut the door and retraced her steps back down the stairs and out through the kitchen.

In the garden, moving gingerly so as not to jostle her shoulder, she set to work feeding the crows. Rosemary was grateful the birds hadn't become offended by her recent proximity to their nesting spot. It gave her hope they might learn to tolerate Jack now that he had agreed to accept a part-time post as the new gardener.

Rosemary watched the smaller crow hop over to her

mate and reach her neck out to be preened. Responding, the male puffed his breast out with pride as he satisfied the request. Bonded, each avian mate instinctively gave the other what was needed without ego or expectation getting in the way. A simple moment of acceptance and care with no jostling for control. Why did humans always complicate things by thinking about them too hard?

It caused Rosemary to wonder. Was Max to be her mate? Were they meant to be together for the rest of their lives? Part of her felt absolutely certain he was. She could almost see the angel on her shoulder urging her to commit to Max, and she knew they might live a long and happy life together.

On her other side, the devil whispered words of doubt. Would Max ever be able to accept her for who she really was? Could he learn to live with her tenaciousness, or would he forever try to make her into something she simply wasn't?

Did she even know who she was now? She certainly felt different than she had when Andrew was alive. Which version of herself did Max truly fancy? These were the questions that had been floating around her mind for some time, questions she didn't know how—or even if—she wanted answered.

The soft sounds of footsteps on the terrace interrupted Rosemary's reverie. When she looked over, she saw

Abigail Redberry walking across the flagstones. "Hello. I—I wanted...I was worried about you, and then I saw you out here and...I hope it's all right?"

"Of course," Rosemary said, finding herself feeling just as flustered as Abigail sounded. She didn't say anything but instead looked expectantly at her neighbor. After all, whatever problem lay between them, it hadn't, to Rosemary's knowledge, been her doing.

Abigail flushed but when she spoke, her voice was clear and sincere. "I owe you an apology. I should never have let my imagination—and the papers—get my head twisted around. You've been nothing but a loyal friend to me. You even helped clear Martin's name when he was accused of murder!"

Choosing her words carefully, Rosemary asked one simple question because she could see that Abigail had already engaged in much self-flagellation, and frankly, she'd heard quite enough fraught explanations recently.

"Was it you who sold me out to the press?"

If it was possible, Abigail's complexion turned ruddier. "Of course not," she insisted, not quite as convincingly as Rosemary would have liked.

She could have pressed, demanded to know how Abigail could have done such a thing, but she would have been a hypocrite. Desperate people did desperate things; in fact, Rosemary had begun to wonder exactly what she was capable of ever since she'd held Briony

Keller's life in her hands and contemplated letting her fall from the church belfry.

Still, she didn't think her relationship with Abigail would be the same going forward, but she also wasn't one to hold a grudge—she was no crow!—and so Rosemary accepted the apology and allowed Abigail to retreat through the hedges.

She sat at the terrace table and looked out onto the garden for a long while after Abigail had gone. Eventually, Frederick found her there and went to fetch Vera. With Wadsworth's help, he settled her onto the outdoor sofa. She and Rosemary watched contentedly while he tossed Dash's rope toy back and forth across the lawn until Desmond arrived a short while later. "Don't leave us guessing, mate. How'd it go?" Frederick asked after Desmond received assurance both Rosemary and Vera were doing quite well, indeed.

Desmond sat down and shook his head as if dazed. "She left it all to me," he said incredulously, having just come from the highly anticipated reading of his aunt's will. "Mother and Father were shocked, though I can hardly fathom why given the way they treated her all these years. Guess they never understood the concept of *you catch more flies with honey*. Of course, I won't let them starve, far from it. However, I believe I'll let them stew on it for a while."

"Well deserved, old friend," Frederick said in

congratulations. "Now, what are you going to do with it all?"

"How should I know?" Desmond asked, bewildered still. "What would you do, Freddie? Buy a villa in the tropics? Blow it all on dames and horses? Pursue your dreams of world domination?"

Frederick whipped the rope toy so hard it almost ended up in Abigail's garden and broke into a wide grin. "Des old boy, you're positively brilliant. That's exactly what we'll do! Vera, darling, wouldn't you fancy testing out that southern accent; see if your dialect really is up to snuff?"

Vera stared at him curiously, but Rosemary had a sneaking suspicion she knew precisely what her brother had in mind. Her eyes met his, and she smiled.

"Mother will be positively furious."

Made in United States
Orlando, FL
29 November 2021

10860954R00157